"SPLIT SCREAM has something for everyone. Gómez offers a haunting of bleak hopes and grim specters, where every sentence breathes a fresh ghost story. Lopes da Silva scratches another itch with their fast-paced conflict of demanding modern milieu and gut-churning body horror. An entrancing duet of nightmare."

—Hailey Piper, Bram Stoker Award-winning author of *Queen of Teeth*

"The combined stories are a beautifully organic Latinx experience. Both are very different in writing style and storyline, however, each kept me wanting more. Cynthia Gomez does a fantastic job with the tale of La Llorona. I loved everything from the characters to the development of the mythology. Fresh takes on oral tradition are a must read for me. M. Lopes da Silva slides into your imagination like a French kiss. This story is delicious and terrifying as it takes you to literal depths you won't expect! And yes to more non-binary writers and characters in horror. Great duo of stories I hope you will check out."

—V. Castro, author *The Queen of The Cicadas* and *Goddess of Filth*

PRAISE FOR "THE SHIVERING WORLD" by CYNTHIA GÓMEZ

"*The Shivering World* empathizes with people pushed to the margins and left with little choice but to lash out. Exploring the monstrosity of both humans and supernatural beings, Gómez fills every page with a quiet, aching dread."

—Eric Raglin, author *Extinction Hymns*

PRAISE FOR "WHAT ATE THE ANGELS" by M. LOPES DA SILVA

"In *What Ate the Angels*, the physically toxic and romantically toxic collide. Lopes da Silva's bizarre body horror story is at once grotesque and tender in its exploration of messy queer love."

—Eric Raglin, author *Extinction Hymns*

SPLIT SCREAM

VOLUME TWO

Featuring:

CYNTHIA GÓMEZ

&

M. LOPES DA SILVA

SPLIT SCREAM
Volume Two

Dread Stone Press
dreadstonepress.com

First Edition: November 2022

ISBN: 978-1-7379740-4-8 / Paperback Edition
ISBN: 978-1-7379740-5-5/ eBook Edition

For the love of horror, and all you weird ones.

INTRODUCTION

T he novelette has been dismissed and disparaged. Some dictionaries don't even define them as a unique form, listing only short stories, novellas, or novels. Others write them off as being "too sentimental" or "trivial".

This is silly, of course, and, with little effort it's easy to see the novelette has a purpose and value.

What makes a novelette, then? Exact word counts vary, but these stories are longer than a short story and shorter than a novella. Entertainment consumable in about an hour or two.

Sound like another form of easily digestible entertainment?

I'm not saying a novelette is a movie is a novelette. And I'm not saying written fiction *needs* to be like movies. But… But they are *kind of* like movies, right? If you're willing to accept that premise, at least for the moment, may I present to you…

SPLIT SCREAM
A Novelette Double Feature

Truly, what better way to present these stories than as a double feature? Do you *have* to read them back to back in a single Friday night after dusk? Certainly not. But could you? Absolutely.

So, what do you say?

You'll first find yourself in a world of poverty and gentrification in Cynthia Gómez's "The Shivering World." There's hope, though, provided you're willing to accept the supernatural and make a sacrifice or two—La Llorona has a way of being convincing. Then, let the oily goop of underground L.A. seep into your brain, courtesy of M. Lopes da Silva's "What Ate the Angels." But it's not just body horror; there's love there, too.

Well, are you ready? Grab some popcorn, turn the lights low, and don't be afraid to scream.

This is Volume Two of the *Split Scream* series. If you read Volume One, my heartfelt thanks to you for coming back. If not, I do hope you enjoy, and that you seek out more.

Long live the novelette!

Alex Ebenstein
Dread Stone Press
Michigan, USA
September 2022

CONTENTS

THE SHIVERING WORLD
Cynthia Gómez

I.

T he signs were falling off the trees around the house
Nayeli hated. *SE BUSCA*, they read, and some also
read *MISSING*. Messages scrawled in the margins: *te
queremos*; *please come home*. Dates reaching back two years,
seven months, four months; grainy pictures faded from the
sun. One man had an American flag tattooed on his shoulder, at his belt buckle the Mexican flag. Some of them were
undocumented, her Uncle César pointed out as he showed
her family around, so they probably just went home. That
explanation made little sense to Nayeli, but by now she was
used to the stories adults told themselves, to seeing the
threads they didn't want pulled.

The strip of water behind the house was called
Courtland Creek, but that name was a joke. When Nayeli
was growing up she and her mother Vero and her younger
brother Mateo used to go up to Temescal Creek on weekends—when the car was working and Vero felt like getting
out of bed. It cut its way down from the hills and

murmured to itself while they ate cheese sandwiches by the muddy banks. She could imagine it running down to the bay and making its way beyond to the ocean. What ran behind the house was just God spitting, Vero liked to say. Water was powerful in any form, was Mateo's response. Nayeli just thought it looked weak.

So the creek wasn't a creek and this house wasn't a home, but after they got evicted from the place on Fruitvale it was where they could go. César had gotten partway to converting the garage before he ran out of money. Most nights the windows smeared over with frost and they piled on his Raiders blankets and slept in knit caps. Daisy-chained extension cords powered a space heater that smelled of burnt hair. Nayeli and her mother shared the sofa bed, and Mateo had an airbed on the floor. It leaked slowly every night and he would wake up with the gray rug under his cheek.

Nayeli worked at the coffee shop on Laney's campus, usually swing shift, after class. The coffee smell lay thick on her hair and in her clothes. When her mother was feeling playful she'd nuzzle Nayeli's hair, slick as black oil and smelling of Antigua or Java or places none of them would ever go.

Twice. That was how many times she'd been more than an hour from home. Once Vero's boyfriend and two of his friends took her and Vero and Mateo to Santa Cruz on their motorcycles. The three men were from the East Bay Dragons: Black men on Harleys, something Nayeli had thought was as unlikely as Black cowboys, until they told her those existed too. The wind whipped the long hair that poked out from under her helmet, and a week later she was still finding sand in her clothes.

Her senior year her boyfriend Josh had taken her to visit the University of Oregon, where his parents had met. His dad helped her with the admissions forms, and it was the only school she finished the application for. But the financial aid application threw Vero into a funk for days, and in the end what Nayeli couldn't leave blank she just made up.

She'd wanted to break up with Josh before the trip, but she could never have paid for it on her own. They hotboxed his lime-green Passport the whole way up and giggled about cutting school to go visit college. She almost wanted to keep him. But sex that night was empty and sad, like the word *damp*. What stopped her from pushing him off was the sound outside their window, of bikes in the rain, and she let herself imagine those wheels underneath her, cutting through puddles and speeding her off to read Anzaldúa in some coffee shop, cedars dripping outside. Three days in Eugene showed her maybe a dozen Latinos. All but two of those were chopping or sweeping or scrubbing, the verbs Nayeli associated with her own kind.

The news came into their inboxes two days after they got back. She'd been accepted; he hadn't. She let herself imagine, for a second, those books, the soft green of the sweatshirts, the bright yellow *O* across her chest. But then she saw the letter offering a tiny scholarship and $40,000 a year in loans. All those zeroes made her pull out her phone and enroll at Laney before she could change her mind.

Mateo had finished school but was still working at Home Depot, where the manager pretended not to notice his long lunch breaks. When he was still in school he'd clamored to be assigned any reports on dams, bridges, anything about taming water or the earth itself. But the night before his tests he would slip off to a sideshow or go smoke weed by the lake. He reminded her of Vero, and Nayeli wanted to shake him for it. Her brother was like one of those air puppets outside the car dealerships, blowing any way the wind would pull it but never leaving the ground.

After a month at Uncle César's she and Mateo saw another sign, the ink reading *SE BUSCA* still fresh and bright. A very young man, long hair in a leather clip, crooked teeth grinning into the wrinkled face of a baby girl. Gone home, she imagined, or maybe dead. She pictured that mouth frozen open, blood running in a thin stream. A thin creek. The missing men were now four.

When they told their mother about this Vero said to them both: "You so much as look at that creek after dark and I'll forget I don't believe in hitting kids."

She liked to say stuff like this, just as she liked to pull down her old books from her only year at Laney and make her kids read her worn volumes of Cherríe Moraga or Audre Lorde, Mateo slipping his phone between the pages, Nayeli scribbling notes in the margins. What Vero left unmentioned were the days she lay glued to whatever soft surface was left in the house, whatever house they were in. They'd come home from school to find Lauryn Hill blasting from her headphones, sometimes Héctor Lavoe. They'd drape a blanket on her shoulders and put a glass of water by her bed. If it was anything by Chavela Vargas they knew to pretend they hadn't seen her at all.

The garage room sat underneath Uncle César's living room and extended partway under the front stairs, so every time he or his family came or went the peeling steps would rattle practically over their heads. It had a single curtained window they could look through to see car crashes, Fourth of July fireworks, a couple having sex by the creek. Their neighbor picking up pans, dishes, shoes, and throwing them at the girlfriends who passed through every few weeks or so. One woman left after a month, the next a few days; once they saw him pulling a woman out of his Camaro a week after she'd tried to leave. Nayeli caught the woman's eye, the skin swelling red even as the door trapped her back inside.

Nayeli was in her second year at Laney and she had by now gotten used to tapping off papers for school on her phone when work was slow, the *A*'s landing on them with no effort. In class she only half-listened, waiting for her classmates to make connections that seemed screamingly obvious. Meanwhile, she doodled in the margins of her notebooks: cedar trees dripping onto damp earth, buds curled behind leaves, waiting to bloom. She could always spot the students who swore they were going to transfer from Laney to a four-year school. The longing came off of them in waves. They were like her friends' parents who promised they were going back to their ranchos in Mexico someday, even as the days stretched into weeks and the weeks into decades. Sure they were. Sure she would.

Then came a night in November with rain in sheets, in Nayeli's hand the first *A* she'd ever sweated for. The assignment had tugged at her, hard: "Tell us a story or a legend you heard growing up. Who told it to you? And why?"

Her mother hadn't been much for bedtime stories, but when she did indulge her children, she loved to frighten them with tales from her own childhood in Juárez. Those tales, Nayeli would later come to realize, were one of the few things from that life her mother had chosen to keep. La Llorona, sometimes Juana in Vero's version, waited at night on the banks of the Río Bravo with her black rebozo and an appetite for wayward children. Juana had killed her children to be with her white lover, was how Vero told it, and was cursed to wander forever, crying their loss. Nayeli knew these stories were meant to scare her, but she mainly wanted to know whether La Llorona ever made it to California.

She'd borrowed the house laptop to write this paper, letting the messages from Vero and Mateo stack up in her phone. She hid out at the main library, telling work she was sick and praying nobody would walk in and see her surrounded by books in piles and sticky notes she'd swiped from the librarian. She scribbled notes in the margins of the library books and folded down the pages and left most of them spread on the table at the end of the day. And now the paper was back in her hand, praise scrawled in green marks. Professor Luna had also written a long email that Nayeli kept opening to read and re-read: an invitation to visit a class at Berkeley, a nudge to think far ahead to next fall when she could apply to transfer there. The word "transfer," always rickety and dull to Nayeli's ears, now sounded like a rope hissing into a well.

The green ink seemed to glow in the gathering dark as she waited for the 40, reading and re-reading the lines that Dr. Luna had marked with a star: "In seeking to forever cut off the line of her own Indian blood, Juana was seeking to cross her own border and plant her feet firmly in the white world where her lover had come from. For her, the dream was of mobility, and her children were the price to pay. In this way, she is a freak mirror image of women like my grandmother, who left her children behind in Juárez for years, in order to come here and give them a better life. The knife that Juana stuck in her children landed in her own heart. My grandmother wanted to protect her own children from a world not so very different from Juana's, but her leaving was a wound of its own kind, and her children have never healed."

Getting home that night took Nayeli so much longer than she'd imagined. Her coworker Jasmín had flaked on a ride, the 40 took forever to come, and when it finally spilled her back out on the street, the rain was much worse. Stomping soaked feet in puddles the last few blocks to home she prayed the green would hold until she could show it to her mother. She felt like she should be wearing pigtails and carrying a SpongeBob backpack. She shivered past the creek where the water slicked the tree roots like oil and for just a second the dark seemed to grow thicker and move. Her head cocked, soaked feet paused, but she turned her head forward and marched on. Past the driveway where the men hoisted cars on jacks and liked to leer at Nayeli as she walked. Past the little yellow house where the neighbor pulled his escaping girlfriends back through the door. Up to the side door to the garage, the rain finally easing up, the clouds parting but grouped in black, as if holding their breath, puffed up and coiled. Waiting.

On the doorknob was Vero's bright pink scrunchie. A fucking scrunchie. The sound of the sofa bed banged against the wall and Nayeli yanked her hand away from the pink as if it were a snake.

She knew Uncle César and her aunt and cousins were upstairs, but knocking on their door would open a flood of questions, and she'd end up defending Vero against all of them. She started back the way she had come, intending to ride the 40 until it was safe to come home. She passed the creek again and remembered Vero's words, her weak warning—*You so much as look at that creek after dark ...*

As she stepped closer the shadows seemed to ripple, as if they had layers. A glass bottle clattered under her foot and into the water below. The light of her phone showed scraps of cardboard and an old crate that she propped against the split oak tree and sat on, her sweatshirt a cushion, and she leaned back against the bark, willing her mind to grow as quiet and dark as the shadows above.

"What are you doing?" The voice came from above Nayeli's head. It sounded like barbed wire scraping against itself. She stumbled to her feet and the crate clattered away.

Where the tree began to reach gently over the bank, a woman's body stretched along the trunk. Her long hair wrapped itself around the tree and into the ground, as if growing out of it. The streetlights barely penetrated here, but Nayeli could see clearly. Rich brown skin, darker than Nayeli herself. Cheekbones high and strong, eyebrows thick. Her eyes looked like black grapes left to dry in the sun. But her mouth was red and wet as a pomegranate, and when it opened red teeth fell out and scattered over the damp ground. She was speaking Spanish, which Vero had tried so many times to teach her children, but Nayeli understood every word.

"Aren't you cold, Nayeli?"

Red teeth on black dirt. Nayeli's tongue lay heavy as wood in her mouth. The woman's hands reached out to stroke Nayeli's bare arms, and they softened in spite of her, expecting the warmth. The hands were so cold that Nayeli jerked away.

"What the fuck?" A line of blisters was forming along Nayeli's forearms.

15

An impish smile.

"I'm sorry. I never get to play jokes. The others screamed or they froze or they prayed. All came out the same. One died just as soon as he saw me. Why not you?"

"Well, I'm either dreaming or somebody slipped me some acid, so I might as well talk to you."

This time the hands were hot as an iron, pinning Nayeli's shoulders to the oak, and even if she'd had the courage to pull away something told her not to.

"You go see what your arms show you tomorrow, then you tell me if you were dreaming or if some drug did this."

The hands cooled and dropped away. She could see the red marks forming on her shoulder even in the dark, the shape of long fingers. The swollen creek dripped. The woman pulled her hair out of the ground, wrapped it around Nayeli. It was smooth and hard as polished wood, and so heavy it forced Nayeli to her knees. The woman knelt too, and Nayeli's eyes wanted to close but she forced them open. If these were her last seconds alive, she wanted to see. She took a breath.

"Are you going to let me go?"

"You? Yes. Far away."

"Where did you come from?"

The black eyes grew shiny and sharp, like onyx.

"Juárez."

"Are you real?"

"You tell me."

The woman stared at her, light that came from nowhere glittering off her eyes. Her hands slid over Nayeli's face.

"Why did you come here, Nayeli?"

The black eyes leaned in.

"I don't know."

"Are you escaping something?"

You have no idea, Nayeli wanted to laugh, but her chest only thudded against the black strands, now tangled and slimy and smelling like stale water. Her eyes were so wide, they hurt.

The woman dangled a pen in front of Nayeli's face, one of those old-fashioned quill pens. The ink was dark green.

"Aren't you trapped, little fox? Do you want out?"

Now Nayeli did laugh, a short bark. "My whole life is a trap. No way out."

"Oh, yes." The onyx dulled again. "Yes, there is." She slipped the pen between Nayeli's trembling fingers. It had no weight at all. "Do you want out?"

"Yes."

As soon as the word hit the air, the strands parted and Nayeli fell to the ground. For a long moment there was nothing but her racking coughs and the shining hair as it braided and unbraided itself.

The woman pulled aside her black rebozo. A belt buckle flashed the colors of the Mexican flag at her waist, the name *Rodolfo* etched in copper. From a shadow in her skirt she drew a tiny photo of a young man with long hair, smiling down at a baby girl. From her mouth came a leather hair clip, *Mario* carved into the skin.

"I'm so cold, Nayeli. Bring me somebody to keep me warm."

Again that sound of barbed wire in the woman's voice as she stroked the leather clip.

"What's your name?"

"Don't you know it, little fox?"

"Aren't you supposed to be weeping?"

Again that impish smile.

"That's a myth."

She pressed Nayeli's lips to hers, tasting of copper and salt. Their cold opened up a row of blisters along Nayeli's mouth.

Nayeli had no memory of walking home, and only knew where she was when she saw the pink scrunchie on the ground. The lines on her arms throbbed. Vero was singing to herself in the shower, from "Suavemente." When she emerged, Nayeli was curled under the blankets, pretending to sleep.

The next day she hid in the back of class to keep everyone from seeing her mouth, kept her long sleeves on at work, even as she mopped the coffee shop floor, cheeks running with sweat. On break, Jasmín pulled out a bag of black grapes, and Nayeli ran to the bathroom to retch. She realized right then where she'd seen that belt buckle, that leather clip. When she got home she opened the sofa bed and crawled across it fully clothed. *SE BUSCA.* Any time her mind softened, reaching for sleep, the phrase jolted her awake like a live wire. She pulled the Raiders blanket over her head, but the phrase was rattling inside it. *SE BUSCA.* And then from outside, a woman's voice rose in a scream.

Wind rattled the window. The scream formed into words: "Please stop, J.J., please." Vero and Mateo were out. No one was there to hear the breaking voice beg. No one, except the whole neighborhood, who must be hearing everything she could, and yet nobody threw open a door, no one shouted into the darkness, "Ma'am, you okay?" The blanket did nothing to keep that voice away. "J.J., please, let's just get inside. Please." You should listen to her, Nayeli wanted to tell him. Maybe you wouldn't go beating on women if you'd met the one who lives right there.

Was that the thought that pulled her upright and into the cold? Her shoes barely on her feet, the blood pounding thick in her ears, her nails digging into her palms—something she wouldn't even realize until later when she saw the marks. The street lights were out. The screams were whispers now as she crossed into the darkness underneath the split oak.

"Stop, J.J., please, let's go inside so you can calm down. Please. Please." The voice came from the other side of the tree. This was the man who pulled women from his Camaro. The man who thought shoes were for throwing at a woman's jaw.

And Nayeli could do what, exactly? Her own fists impotent, tiny, the delicate bones. Her blisters throbbed. "Where are you now, whatever your name is?" Nayeli whispered. *This man will keep you warm*, she thought. *You can eat him raw.*

There wasn't anyone with Nayeli, and then there was. There was the hair sliding around the tree above Nayeli's head, and the voice, not sounding like wire or metal at all; it purred, soft as black silk. As hair braiding itself around a slim neck. Pomegranate teeth fell to the dirt.

"Do you need me, Nayeli?"

"Who the hell is that?"

The voice wasn't J.J., but his girlfriend or whoever was on the other end of his fists. Nayeli stepped around the tree and made herself look, by the light that didn't come from the dead streetlights, the light that shouldn't have been there at all.

The girlfriend was on the ground. Nayeli didn't know humans could look like that. There'd been a face once, and there would be again. She could see the shadow of it hidden inside the swollen cheekbones, the jaw streaked with blue. The eyes buried in all that hurt weren't grateful, weren't bathing Nayeli in relief. They glared.

"Leave us alone," his girlfriend's voice squeezed out from a swelling throat. From behind Nayeli came the smell of rotten water, warm copper and salt. J.J.'s hands came up, soft and open, as if to swat Nayeli away.

"Go home, you dumb bitch. This ain't your business."

"The fuck it isn't, pendejo."

"Didn't I warn you?"

What was this, some tired movie on her abuela's TV? Where did men talk like that? Nayeli saw him gather a fist, arm pulled taut, body coiled and ready, yet calm, like there was nothing to keep him from swinging the fist into her face, maybe her throat—nothing except the long braid that slid from around the trunk and wrapped itself around his wrist.

No screams or breaking voices now. The rebozo muffled his mouth and the strands of long hair pulled him to the ground, gleaming black handcuffs. His girlfriend didn't move, just stared through swollen eyes, like she was already gone and had only left her body sitting on the ground. Maybe she had.

"You should leave now. And you should forget," Juana whispered into the woman's ear. When she crawled away she left knee-shaped indentations in the mud, and did not look back. Like she was afraid they'd turn her into a pillar of salt.

As Nayeli stared at the form on the ground she thought of all the times she'd been powerless. That sick roiling in her chest when she was nine and a boyfriend of Vero's came back after Vero kicked him out, rattling the windows and the doors while Vero huddled in the bathtub with her children, baseball bat in her hand.

Nothing. That was all Nayeli could ever do. Until now, this body lying before her, trussed as a chicken. She knelt down beside it.

"You want to hit me now, pendejo? Maybe call me a bitch?" The words tasted sour and wonderful in her mouth, like plum candy. Juana's eyes met hers. Polished onyx, edges glowing deep red.

"You're done giving bruises." A line that belonged nowhere but a movie. She smacked his face, but so lightly, just to show that she could. Fear widened his eyes.

"Don't worry, J.J. I'm not like you. I don't beat up people who can't fight back."

His mouth had been still and now it strained under the rebozo. She pulled away the cloth.

"You're acting like everybody don't do this."

"Liar. Good men don't hit women. Your girlfriend didn't know what you were until it was too late, right?

None of them knew. Would anybody pick you if they knew what you do?" She had an image, so delicious she actually had to shift her thighs slightly apart. She slid the rebozo back over his mouth, pulled it tight.

"Imagine if every bruise you ever gave showed up on you instead. Imagine how that would look."

The pomegranate mouth grinned.

Below the rebozo a patch began to grow, the color of a plum, the shape of a fist. Another on his cheekbone, swelling so thick that it swallowed his eye. Another spread over his throat, where his white-gold cross glittered. He began to choke. More bruises bloomed on his arms, his chest. He tried to scream through the black cloth but his throat was swelling shut. The onyx eyes locked on hers, and nowhere in Nayeli's head or behind her lips could she find the words to make it stop. Maybe they'd never been there at all.

So she watched his entire body turn gleaming maroon, then lose all its form, pooling and soaking into the earth. A few thin streams ran down the sloped bank, and she knew there was no way she could have heard the drops hit the creek, but later her memory would tell her she had.

She would remember sobbing until her voice gave out, and the burning hands pulling her to her feet. But she would never remember who shoved the cross into her pocket, or that before she staggered nearly blind back to the house the silky voice sighed a thank you, and then La Llorona settled herself back into the dark.

II.

D ays went by and no one put up any signs for J.J. Any time steps neared the garage door Nayeli stiffened, expecting someone with his picture and a list of questions, but no one came. The only signs that went up were hung on his door, demanding the rent, and after weeks of notices a crew came to prepare the house for sale. They covered up the yellow paint with gray and ripped the nopales from the yard.

She started going the long way around to avoid the creek, afraid of meeting again the girl she'd been that night, when a single wish out loud meant a man erupting into bruises only to disappear. Nights meant lying in the quiet of her family's sleeping breaths to sob without sound, taking care never to jostle the sofa bed or the air mattress just beneath.

One night, the second in a row with no sleep at all, she slid the covers aside and sat up straight in the dark. Her mother was stretched on her side, faded sweatshirt rising and falling, steady in a way her waking self never was.

Nayeli sucked in a long breath and began: "Mami, there's something I have to tell you. I have to tell you and you won't understand."

But on the floor she heard blankets rustling and the light of Mateo's phone lit up his face. She could see only his eyes, blacker than she'd ever seen them and fixed on her. The silence between them felt both thinner and heavier than she'd ever felt in her life. Like she could peel it away from the corner of the room and find the shivering world just beneath. Or like it could press her flat and still, eyes fixed on the ceiling, no way to move. The air alive and crackling, the two of them alone against their mother's absence. Like always. Don't leave me, his still body might be saying. Wherever you're going, don't leave me. Or maybe it was nothing more than a warning: this won't go the way you think it will.

Nayeli lay back down and brought the blanket up to her chest, holding very still until Mateo's face went dark. She raised a shaking finger to her mother's back, the soft cotton smelling of Suavitel, where she traced a word, then another. The light touch seemed to lull her mother further into sleep, and Nayeli had traced the last of her confession on her mother's back when the sun came up.

That morning she stumbled onto the 40, head aching worse than it ever had but somehow lighter, as if she had hollowed it out. In the aisle she tripped over the outstretched legs of a man who sat with an arm fully encircling his girlfriend's neck, his body between hers and the door. The woman's eyes were fixed out the window, nothing of hers choosing to touch him but his entire body clasping hers. Nayeli had seen this couple before, but today as she stared at the man's impassive face she imagined she could see right through it. She saw J.J.'s face floating in maroon just behind this man's skin, and she wondered what a visit to the creek would do to him, what story this man's body would tell. She felt the cross grow warmer in her jacket pocket and warmer still as she slipped it around her neck, and she lifted her eyes to all the men huddled in their seats. She imagined the curtains lifting on every single face, and her pulse began thrumming against the white gold. She forced herself to stand, to yank the cord and jump off the bus into the cold, walking the last ten blocks to class.

On a chilly night at the end of that week Nayeli was warming up her mother's favorite, leftover carrot soup from the coffee shop, the hints of ginger and fennel crowding out the smell of the damp, when an email came in from

Dr. Luna. She'd found a class for Nayeli to visit, the first day of the spring semester. If the visit went well she could audit the class, a step toward proving to Berkeley that it was where she belonged. "You have a promising future, Nayeli," Dr. Luna wrote. *Future.* The word sounded shiny and bright and she imagined polishing a stone to bring out what glimmered underneath. Or digging through mud to find a flash of silver. Maybe a white-gold cross.

That was when the door opened wide to the jangle of Vero's keys and a blast of cold air and, just behind it, something familiar—a sharp, lemony cologne. Nayeli's hands clenched into fists as she realized who'd brought it into the room.

His name was Chris, and he'd first come around when they were living on East 15th Street but was gone before Courtland Avenue. He had a house in Hayward they could never visit, an adult son he never called. But he could coax Vero off the couch when nobody else could, and somehow in his presence Uncle César bit his preaching tongue. Chris was a cook at a senior care home, where they kept him in the kitchen so the residents wouldn't see his arms and neck, covered in tattoos. He'd taken Mateo and Nayeli there once, telling them they'd better never abandon Vero in a place like that. While he spoke he stared at Nayeli's breasts.

Vero was never alone now. Chris was there the day Vero lost another job, and Nayeli wasn't sure who she wanted to hit more: Vero or him. Again? The only way Nayeli could see out of these damp walls was to stay in them long enough to finish school, to transfer out. It was a rotten-wood cage, and Vero kept acting like she wanted to burn it up.

That night she and Chris sat on the sofa, him rubbing her shoulders as she filled out job applications online. Nayeli couldn't watch, couldn't stand the flutters of hope in her own chest whenever Vero called out a good lead. She could almost see, behind Vero, a shadow in the room, the woman Vero had wanted to become. Vero had spent a year at Laney, had begun growing a dream of transferring to Berkeley. A lawyer, she had imagined herself, maybe eventually a judge, fair and kind and tough to all who stood before her perfectly ironed robes. But that dream snapped in two when she got pregnant with Nayeli before the end of her first year. Every house they moved to, even this little room, Vero lugged around her Laney books, their faded yellow stickers peeling and threatening to fall off. Nayeli couldn't shake the thought that she knew Vero, and she knew her mother, but she'd never get a chance to meet the woman who'd been growing inside those books, inside those pages, inside the very same orange chairs that held Nayeli three mornings a week. *You should've got an abortion*, Nayeli thought as she regarded Vero's crumpled face.

It got worse. One night in December, the end of the semester less than ten days away, Nayeli was hunched over the laptop, working on a paper for Dr. Luna's class. All around her were the books she kept nearby almost every waking minute now, names like López and Talamante and Alarcón, as if somehow she could make a wall between herself and the creek if she piled them up high enough. Mateo had just handed her the vape pen when they heard two sets of footsteps rattling the porch and a fist knocking on Uncle César's door. The thick boots and booming voice belonged to the landlord, Paul; behind him in clicking heels came his wife, Nancy. The voices were low and they had to fight to hear over the sound of a leaf blower outside, but what they heard was enough—*assessor, valuation, right of access, notice to vacate. Courtesy visit.* Words that softly rustled, hiding the violence inside, a mallet wrapped in silk.

Nayeli peeked through the curtain to see Nancy standing in front of the eagle and serpent painted on César's garage door. "I still think you're selling too soon. And why do you *only* rent to illegals?"

Paul didn't bother lowering his voice. "They scatter easier."

Two days later came a pair of engineers to review the foundation. The assessor was next, and the day after that a contractor, tracing and measuring the single-paned windows, the dirt and mold smudging onto his hands. At the end of that week Nayeli was trudging home after a final exam, every window in the house curtained and dark, and Paul himself was standing on the porch, holding a white envelope that seemed to glow in the porch light. He half-jumped when he saw her and clutched the paper a bit tighter in his hand.

"It's a formal notice. I'll be listing the house starting Monday. You should expect open houses the following weekend."

He slipped the envelope under the doormat and Nayeli felt her rope, chopped in two, free-falling to the bottom of the well. When he hit the bottom step he found her standing there, blocking his path.

"My uncle said you were maybe going to wait until June. My cousin's almost done with high school. Please don't make her start over now." She couldn't stand the way her voice spiraled higher and thinner with every word.

"That's why I took the trouble to come here in person. I wanted to find your aunt and uncle at home."

"Fuck you. You wanted to slip that under the mat and not see any of us."

His face flushed pink.

"Please, we don't have anywhere else to go."

The blush spread to his jaw, but he said nothing and slid between Nayeli and the porch, headed back to the Prius he'd parked ten steps from the creek.

She followed behind his departing back, not knowing why she was bothering but realizing only that she hated him—for thinking his shame and red face would absolve him, for the shiny cufflinks he couldn't stop fidgeting with and that probably cost more than their month's rent, for the ring of keys at his waist, each leading to a family that he could make scatter with a click of a mouse or a flick of a pen. Invisible faces that meant nothing to him.

"You don't see us. You've never seen us."

This made him glance back, the pink nearly gone, and worse was what she saw just underneath, the reflexive embarrassment sliding away like a metal grate. Nothing left but annoyance. *Why aren't you scattering?* His face seemed to say.

She could feel the white gold heating up against her chest. *Make him see you, little fox,* scraped the voice inside her head, metal on metal, rust falling in flakes. She'd worked so hard to stay away from where that voice lived, and now it was right here, and nobody was home in the dark houses behind her, nobody to see if the silk braid choked off his breath. Nobody but him to see the shivering world that had always lain right here, curled inside her breastbone, stretched around a split oak.

And then the creek began to swell. It was rushing with the waters of Temescal Creek, of the Río Bravo, rapids swirling around black rocks. The rapids were choked with drowning men. Each was weighed down by the sign around his neck, black lettering that read *ALIEN*. The bodies had no faces, only brown skin. They climbed the bank and reached for Paul and his eyes locked on hers, disbelief collapsing into terror, hands scrabbling into empty air.

You couldn't see me before? Nayeli thought as the brown arms pulled him under. *None of us? You couldn't see my mother, the slivers of hope she still keeps, the funhouse mirror she holds onto for seeing herself with? My brother, who adapts to anything, the best and the worst thing he knows how to do? My uncle, who stays rigid as wood because he's afraid if he bends he'll never stand upright again? And what about me, still not smothering to death under the boredom, still trying to claw my way out? You're so fucking impatient that we won't get out of your way, and the only other emotion you can manage for us is fear?*

"Then that's what you get." These were the only words she said out loud, and he would never hear them— he was already gone. Nayeli stood very still as the water trickled back to what it had been, then walked to where the red mouth had lain quiet in the shadows.

"Well done, little fox," the voice rasped. Nayeli didn't dare speak. She knew that if she did, she would hear the barbed wire scraping coming from her own mouth, or hear that Spanish could now emerge from her lips without a thought, the way she understood it only when it came from La Llorona, and she would never feel her body go hot or blisteringly cold at the next J.J., the next Paul, the next—

35

"The next who, Nayeli?" The voice was soft now, like the eyes, black and liquid, as if inviting Nayeli to fold herself into the shadows and stay there forever. Yes, the second Nayeli spoke, she would learn who she was, who she'd become. And there would be no more pretending to be the normal girl who skipped class to smoke weed and listened to SZA in a moldy garage.

"Don't lie to yourself, Nayeli. You know who you are. And we both know you didn't call me this time. This was every bit *you*."

The cuff links glittered between them on the ground, and the black eyes shone down, not in a dare, but in a smirk, as if to say they both knew what she would do next, which was to bend down and pull them from the dirt, the silver slippery and cold against the rising heat of her hands. She turned away from the shadows, but she knew they trailed behind her like dark water, like a rebozo she'd thrown over herself. She headed back to the house. She had a letter to retrieve.

III.

Two weeks after Paul disappeared the cops found the Prius blocks away from the house, its windows smashed and stereo gone, seats rotted from the rain. They never came to the door. No contractors either, and Nancy sent a single terse letter, telling César to direct the rent to her, no mention of selling. Three days before New Year's Eve César mailed the check, the whole family holding their breath as the mailbox closed.

January storms swelled the creek, and sometimes Nayeli could feel them at work, the waters rising in her chest and yearning to spill when a customer asked her out then took his tip back from the jar when she said *no*. One night a car full of men drove slowly beside her for blocks as she walked home from the bus stop. She imagined the scummy waters filling their mouths, their tongues silent forever. Their catcalling voices beating inside their own heads, screaming out all other sounds, never a second's peace. She thought again of the man on the bus, of all the men, in buses, in cars, the water pulling back their layers like a bloody curtain. She lifted her eyes to the idling car, the lights stabbing into the dark, and then a horn honked behind it, and the car sped out of her reach.

She started seeing signs of Chris everywhere in the little room: bright yellow sweatshirt on the floor by the shower; Nitro Tech muscle powder on top of the mini-fridge; his black Tundra jutting over the driveway's lip. He was there the day she was supposed to visit Dr. Campos's class at Berkeley, watching her get up four, five, ten times to pull aside the faded curtain and look again for Jasmín's car. Dr. Campos had invited her to a kebab restaurant after class, him and two of his grad students, and a Lyft would have eaten up the money. Every time she checked her phone she opened the ride-share app and closed it again, making herself see those cedar trees she knew would be there, the clipped green lawn, students draped across it and dropping words like *liminality* as casually as they ate their sandwiches.

Finally a text from Jasmín: *Sorry, so scattered today, Im leaving in 5*. Jasmín lived twenty minutes away. It was too late. If she took the bus now she'd catch the last ten minutes of the class.

She looked up to see Chris looming over her, keys dangling, and when he offered a ride she wished more than anything that she could say *no*, a single cold word she could drop over her shoulder while swishing past him on her way to a waiting car, door slamming, motor purring to life under her hands.

Nayeli's memory of that night would forever be tinged with cheap ramen, a smell she hated more than almost anything else in the world. Mateo loved the stuff; her mother ate it only when she was desperate or depressed. She had been pacing, which took some doing in a place that small. As soon as Nayeli walked in the door after Chris dropped her off her mother's face was a war zone. Nayeli knew that war well. On one side, hope lined up, rustling like clean cotton skirts, like book pages. Her babygirl at Berkeley, cap and gown gleaming. The questions stacked behind and inside each other: *How was it? What did you learn? Did you like it there? Are you going to transfer? Did they like you? Was it pretty?* On the other side, lurking, no order, nothing neat or hopeful, were leather-clad soldiers hissing, Vero's own dreams of Berkeley pouring from their mouths, and louder than anything was the clanging chorus from her worried pacing all afternoon: *Where's my man? What were you doing?* The chorus drowned out the obvious questions: *Why are you crying? Are you okay?* This war zone was her mother, split down the middle. The wound that had never healed.

Nayeli ignored her entirely and ducked into the bathroom to change her shirt, the green one, her favorite. The wadded-up ball seemed to hold all the joy of the afternoon.

She heard a tap at the bathroom door. Would it be her mother? The one who, even when they had to leave the shitty apartment on 38th Street, used a coworker's address so they didn't have to transfer out of Tech midyear? Or would it be Vero, who quit that job not even a month later, tight-lipped and defensive when they asked her why they had to transfer after all? Or would it be the shadow that danced between the two, the one who couldn't decide whether to confess or to smirk to her kids the truth: that she'd been fired for spray-painting *keep your hands to yourself* on the coworker's car? That shadow didn't even have a name.

"What the hell were you and Chris doing?"

Vero, then. The one she knew best of all. Nayeli stepped into the room.

Mateo had his headphones on, curled up on the sofa, eyes cast down. Beating behind Nayeli's forehead was the rough skin of Chris's hand, slithering up her thigh as he took her home, the road slipping past her with no way out. His snakelike grin when he slipped his hand back onto the steering wheel, those eyes that told her he could put that hand back any time.

"Mami, I don't think Chris is such a good man for you." The space heater hadn't warmed the room and Nayeli couldn't stop shivering.

"What do you know? All of nineteen. When you get to be my age you'll see how rare a good man is."

Nayeli took in the busted-up microwave rusting in the corner; the carpet molding under their feet; the far-off sound of Uncle César's TV drifting underneath the door. "If he's so great, why's he with you?"

"What did you say to me?"

Mateo's headphones slipped down and Kendrick Lamar shouted into the air. *Why were they just* staring? Nayeli thought. *Why didn't one of them cross the room and slap her?* She bit her lip and tried again.

"Mami, if his life is so great, why is he dating a woman who can't keep a job or an apartment and lives in a garage with her two kids? Why doesn't he show you this nice life he has in store for you? Why doesn't he invite you to his great house so you can sleep in a real bed? Wake *up*! He is playing you and you let him."

And still the silence. This was Vero's couch-face, starting to soften and blur. *Stand up to me!* Nayeli wanted to scream. *Now is when you're supposed to forget you didn't believe in hitting kids,* now is when your hands come up to show where the limits are. Vero had forgotten what her hands were for. Where were her hands all those times Nayeli slipped out at 11 on a school night? Hands that were supposed to yank Nayeli back into whatever ratty chair the kitchen had and make her do that homework, the work so easy it was insulting. Not pulling on headphones so thick she couldn't know where her kids had gone. All those times she and Mateo both had reached out, feeling for their mother's hands to know where the boundary was, where was the limit, the edge, the wall to stay inside of. And finding nothing but empty air. Mateo thrived on the freedom; he swayed back and forth like those stupid air puppets. Nayeli sucked the emptiness inside herself, where it froze. Like Vero's face right now. Nayeli took a breath and tried one more time.

"And he's a fucking asshole!"

If she told it all, would Vero just stand still, like she was doing now? A wax figure of herself, a wooden doll? Would she push that loser boyfriend out of the door and recite Audre Lorde? Or would she tell Audre to *go fuck yourself, you're dead and I have a life?*

Later, Nayeli so wanted to believe that she would have been brave enough to find out. But Vero's answer came anyway, when her hand reached out to slap Nayeli across the jaw.

And it wasn't even to defend herself, but her chosen man.

There was nothing to do but slam the door and storm off into the dark. Leaves crunched as her feet took her to the split oak tree. Above her was the violet sky, behind her the garage door, eagle devouring the serpent, its execution stayed. In the little room was her stack of books, yellow stickers on their spines, a paper due at the end of the week. They would pile up every semester, more papers to write, years left to go. She'd defended the cage from a vulture, only to be trapped in it with a snake. She pressed her head against the oak.

"Such dithering, little fox. It's beneath you now, don't you think?" The black hair was loose and free and sliding itself into Nayeli's hands, smelling of a lemony cologne and a hint of cedar. "Foxes eat snakes in the wild."

When she was ten Nayeli had stolen a nature book from the library and opened it over and over again to a photo near the end, a trap stained red, nothing left inside it but a single fox's paw, fresh with teeth marks. Even then she'd known just what that cold steel would feel like, could taste the blood, warm copper and salt, as her teeth set her free.

"But it's not just me I'll be hurting," she rasped. Barbed wire scraping against itself.

"You know why you came here, Nayeli." The red-rimmed eyes were glowing, showing Nayeli nothing but her own reflection, caged in steel, and her own gnashing teeth, tearing into trapped flesh, a line of blood streaking across the wet earth, looking down to see every piece of herself still intact, and back behind her Vero and Mateo, bodies marked with puncture wounds, staring at Nayeli through matted fur while the steel jaws held them tight.

It took her days to find Chris alone. The night it finally came was windy and cold. Vero was at work and Mateo was at his girlfriend's, and Nayeli opened the door to the fading sound of the vacuum, Chris wrapping up the cord. A woman's voice rose into the silence, singing something about how it would feel to be free. The microwave was warming a macaroni casserole. Chris must have brought it.

She stood in the doorway. He hadn't seen her; she could turn and walk around the block, pretend she could walk back to whoever she had been. She was almost turned around. Almost gone.

"Hey, beautiful."

Or not.

She'd prepared her line, straight out of the kinds of movies Vero loved, the ones with dangerous women who got punished before the credits rolled.

"Can we get out of here?"

He blinked but just barely, as if hardly surprised, and the cross grew hot against her chest.

"Where?"

"I'll show you."

He played with the class ring he always wore on his left hand as the honeyed voice sang, and Nayeli could feel the longing in every breath, as if it were singing out of her own chest.

"Who's that?"

"That's Nina Simone, baby. And it's like she's up in heaven putting on this song just for us."

Us. *Us.* She was young enough to be his daughter. Who the fuck did he think he was? Who did he think *she* was? She could taste the fury again, sour plum, this time with a hint of lemons pickled and dried.

"Let me drive?" She took his keys from the hook before he could say no and wrapped her rebozo around her neck. The door slammed shut.

Plum and eucalyptus leaves made a tunnel overhead as the Tundra, black and immaculate, slipped along the dead-end street at the dark end of the neighborhood, where a culvert swallowed the creek and the smell of pine and cedar bled into the air from a pair of houses being gutted and reconstructed at the top of the bank. The tires slid to a halt and the lights winked off and the windows rolled down in the chill.

"Nayeli. Nayeli." Her mother's voice distorted, like coming through water. Rotten water, shining scales. Nayeli curled on her side. There was no leafy tunnel, no Tundra, only the couch and her mother and Mateo and the moldy garage. She was hot and swollen, slipping around inside her pajamas. The Raiders blanket slid off. Like snakes, sliding through a shallow creek and into a culvert while Nayeli watched, cold and still.

"Keep the blanket on, baby. You've got a fever of 101."

A damp rag on her forehead and an ice cube her mother tried to press to her lips. Nayeli pushed them away.

"When is this?"

Her mother and Mateo glanced at each other before either of them spoke, and her mother kept pausing while she explained. They'd heard rustling, and when they looked through the curtains they saw Nayeli standing motionless in front of the door, eyes fixed on the handle. When they pulled the door open she'd collapsed into her mother's arms. Here Mateo looked straight at Nayeli, his expression fixed and hard in a way she never saw from him, this brother who drifted in the wind. Her mother crossed her arms, but not before Nayeli saw the blisters lining the inside of both.

"You did that." She barely recognized Mateo's voice.

Her mother bit her lip and leaned to replace the blanket over Nayeli's shoulders. "When I carried you in, m'ija, you were really…Um." She bit the edges of a manicured nail.

"You were really cold." Mateo fixed his eyes on the window, the frost layering itself.

"Where's Chris?" Hands reaching out for her from the passenger seat, hands like snakes, that grin like a python's grin stretching his face. Then one snake after another sliding past her and through the open windows, the soft hissing as Chris ceased to exist. And yet she held her breath as if they might say he was out getting pizza, he'd be coming right back.

"I don't want to talk about that now."

"Why?"

"He hasn't texted or called her for two days."

"Anyway, m'ija, don't think about him anymore. We can't ever count on them, can we?"

The hands stroking her forehead smelled of Vicks VapoRub and honey-lemon tea. Warm things, sweet things, perfuming the air. Nayeli wanted to push her mother's hands away, these things she no longer deserved, but the hands were holding her and pressing the cup to her lips and she knew where they were.

Nayeli anonymously reported Chris's truck as abandoned, using a library computer that kept freezing up. *I'm trying to sell my house*, she added, *and things like this lower the property value.* Vero tried for days to reach him, until finally she found his older sister on Instagram. Chris had a fiancé in Antioch and a girlfriend in Hayward but no house, and none of his relatives had spoken to him for years, his daughters included. Vero threw her phone across the room and forbade either of them from saying his name ever again.

Nobody did, but its absence took up all the air in the room. Silences had always held them together, Vero pretending that her children didn't skip school and them pretending not to notice when she was punishing herself with her own mother's favorite songs. This silence was like carbon monoxide, pushing Vero onto the couch every day, slack as a rope and staring at the yellow curtains into nothing; backing Mateo all the way into the corner, bass blaring from his headphones, eyes never landing on Nayeli but their weight at her back all the same. She stayed in class, at the library, anywhere but the little room. Even the tiny backyard might mean Uncle César tending to his azaleas, scouring the leaves for the tiniest hint of rot, smiling and offering her a cup of hot chocolate.

For her final paper in Dr. Campos's class, Nayeli wrote: "The popular image of La Llorona fills us with horror precisely because she crossed a line that women aren't meant to cross. Folklore of her time is full of women as the *victim* of violence, but she became its agent. The myth punishes her, condemning and confining her forever to the darkness, and every time we retell it we condemn her again. But what if she saw that choice as the only way out? We abhor her choice but not how few of them she ever had." Dr. Campos said she could audit as many of his classes as she wanted, but also suggested she rethink the last two lines, his eyes not meeting hers. She remembered the stories he'd told the class, the pictures he'd shown of his youth in Mexico City, some taken in the immaculate house where he'd grown up. The silver tea set, the polished tiles, the Turkish rugs, all of them a net ready to catch him if he ever fell. She played with the class ring in her pocket and said nothing.

That night she dreamed of a ceremony, rows of graduates in lemon-colored robes crowding the banks of the creek, their eyes identical and dull as black grapes. Her mother was in regalia on the stage, reading out every name, and when she called Nayeli's a faceless trio rose up in the crowd and tossed strands of silver and white gold into her path. She froze, knowing that something terrible would happen if she let her feet touch any of it, and she hissed at the trio to take their metal back. "All you ever had to do was leave me alone. Why the fuck didn't you just leave me alone?" On each blank face a pomegranate mouth bloomed into a grin and the other graduates stared at her, diplomas gripped in their hands, paths branching before them, smooth and clear. "How dare you judge me?" she screamed at the black eyes. Finally she let her feet touch the first flash of silver and then she was running, and she turned her face to her mother, but there was no one there. Only a pillar of salt, crumbling and scattering itself over the ground. And a diploma.

By summer Nayeli realized her mother was never coming back. There was only Vero now. Some days she'd be cleaning and re-cleaning to Héctor Lavoe so loud her children could barely think, other days tremulously stepping outside, blinking as if the sun would burn her. César began leaving boxes of food on their door after church, always with a Bible tract that Vero might read aloud, tears streaming, or might crumple into a ball.

One morning in August Nayeli found Vero sitting on the floor holding a set of cufflinks and a black silk rebozo. Nayeli gently tugged them from her trembling hands and they both smelled it, released into the air, a trace of a sharp and lemony cologne. Vero's eyes sought her daughter's, liquid and wide, behind them the connections struggling to knit themselves. Nayeli put the rebozo and cufflinks away without a word, and led Vero's sagging figure back to the couch. She laid on two blankets, extra heavy, and microwaved hot water for tea.

Then came the evening in November when Nayeli left her phone out, open to her Berkeley transfer application. She came out of the shower to find Vero gone and all of Vero's Laney books tossed into the compost bin, stinking and damp. Vero was back at dawn, throat spread over with red marks, cheap beer on her breath, laughter rising into a cackle, higher and higher, as if daring her voice to break. When Nayeli told La Llorona about this she could barely choke out the words. Vero's yellow stickers, those hopeful flags, the weight Vero had carried for so many years. Her mother dissolving into a pillar of salt, the foxes bleeding in their cage. La Llorona traced coal-hot fingernails on the softness of Nayeli's inner arm. The image she branded looked like a crocodile, shedding a tear.

On a sticky afternoon the following May, clouds wavering between dissolving or settling in, Nayeli left Dr. Campos's class and her phone vibrated against her thigh. One email from the admissions office, another from the office that awarded a full scholarship, one so prestigious you couldn't even apply. They were delighted to offer; they would be pleased to welcome. She read the words out loud to no one, and they were warm and soft on her trembling tongue.

She headed for her favorite spot on the Berkeley campus, a stand of trees framing Strawberry Creek. There was a cedar tree draping over the water, the trunk wide enough to let her stretch her body on top and dangle her hair over the bark. She'd found a beautiful rebozo in a shop on International. It was overpriced, but her heart beat faster when she pulled it from the rack. It beat faster now. The clouds were settling in and the turquoise seemed to

glow against the gray. She wrapped the rebozo around her
shoulders and closed her eyes.

WHAT ATE THE ANGELS

M. Lopes da Silva

I n a hollow space behind the crumbling corner of an underground speakeasy that wasn't supposed to exist, something that should not be able to exist stirred, restless. Los Angeles traffic shook the ceiling regularly, sending dust down in rhythmic patters.

The impossible creature moved.

A chunk of concrete fell from a hole in the wall and hit the floor; the sound echoed in the largely empty room. The smell of asphalt gumming in the summer sun came from the corner. From the thing behind the corner. And there was something else. A deep, dull vibration pulsed through the walls—a subaural rhythm radiating out from the thing in the hollow. Faint, but persistent.

Footsteps approached. There was a metallic jangling, scraping, jingling. The eerie rhythm hushed, becoming so soft it could have been mistaken for the passing of traffic above. In the darkness, a rectangle of light wiggled roughly into existence, a human silhouette framed in its center.

"It's probably rats. Don't worry, once we get the construction company in here we can clear all this crap out and put in the underground parking you wanted," said a white man to another, unseen person. He looked for a light switch, groping the walls until he realized there wasn't one. He held his phone up inside the abandoned speakeasy and used its flashlight function, aiming it at the old murals on the walls. Ribald cartoons intertwined with Art Deco grape vines and Greek statuary. He took a few pictures and texted the murals to someone on his phone.

The unseen person's voice faintly called for him. The man looked up from his phone. "Give me a minute! There's a bunch of art on the walls down here. I'm seeing if we can sell it off to somebody—it looks old. How old did the real estate agent say this building was? The thirties?"

Another rock fell from the corner.

The man swept the phone's light in that direction: there was only the broken wall and darkness beyond. But then something in the darkness briefly reflected the phone's light back at him. He squinted.

"What the fuck?"

He opened the camera app on his phone again and tried to zoom in on the shadows, but was met with increasingly distorted digital grain. He grunted. The man glanced down at the steep wooden staircase in front of him and cautiously tested the top step with his weight. The wood audibly complained about his experiment but held. He made his way down.

The thing in the hollow space was alert. Listening without ears. Watching without eyes. Extending, ever so slowly, several long, thread-thin, febrile antennae out from the roiling center of their being.

The man covered his nose with his shirt sleeve; the reek of tar and rot intensified, burning his nose. He held his phone out in front of him. There wasn't much in the underground room besides the murals: a dusty bar along the far wall, a few broken chairs and tables pushed up against the other wall. And the hole in the corner. Where something was glittering.

In one burst of nervous energy the man darted to the hole and shoved his phone inside of it, hardly aware of how hard he was breathing, how fast his heart was beating.

A human skull was inside of the hole. Yellowish. A little dirty.

Seeing it there was almost reassuring; a cheap scare from a 1950s B movie. He took a picture and laughed at himself a little.

His laugh was cut short as the sticky darkness rushed at him, filling him so hotly and quickly his eyes were melting somewhere in the back of his skull while his spine curled backwards and his body crunched into the hole gut-first, his phone clattering to the floor.

In the stillness that followed, the subaural rhythm returned—soft, faint. But within minutes the intensity of its pulse buzzed the walls.

November Martins was eating their girlfriend again. They tried to imagine themself as a giant wolf's tongue, long and red and flat as they hunched over her and recited their lines from the script:

"I hold you in my mouth, but I don't chew, and I don't swallow you yet, because I want to taste you for a while."

Their girlfriend squirmed underneath the red sheet. "Hold me in your mouth," she said, her voice muffled by 400-thread-count.

November tugged a velvet weighted blanket slowly over their girlfriend's body, trying to be more tongue-like in their movements—that was the note they'd gotten from Heather the last time—as they covered her. The blanket was bright red, like most of the décor in Heather's bedroom. November was careful to leave Heather's mouth unvelveted, her breath puffing the sheet with her increased excitement.

"You taste delicious," they said to her. The buzz of a vibrator started emanating from the pile on the bed. November grinned. "My teeth are long and sharp, but they don't harm you."

Heather groaned beneath the fabric and November yearned to tug the sheet away but kept to the script.

"I'm going to swallow you now, are you ready?" they asked.

"Swallow," she echoed in a tiny voice.

They lowered themself so that their chest just met the velvet, and delicately began to slide across her cocooned form. She cried out, ecstatic, and November trembled but kept their arms and legs locked so that their weight didn't fully press down upon her.

"You're going deep inside of me, where it's warm and safe," they said.

Vowels, incoherent and melodic, came from beneath them. November's soft arms burned.

Then they said something off script: "You can hear my heartbeat. It's so close to you."

Heather went quieter, uncertain.

"You're in my stomach, and I'm going to digest you now," they said quickly, back on script again, and gently lowered themself, letting their weight push the writhing, moaning, buzzing mass beneath them into further ecstasies. They pulled their arms around her and the velvet, squeezing tight, tighter, then released her. They did this again and again, like the palpitations of a digesting gut. Until Heather's nervous system lit up like neon and the buzzing stopped and she pulled the sheet free of her white face, gasping, and kissed them.

"Thank you," she said. "Thank you for doing this."

The kissing made November goofy. "You're welcome for doing this."

Heather laughed. "You dork! Do you want to listen?"

"Yes."

Heather pushed the weighted blanket aside and lifted the edge of the sheet up—an invitation. They crept underneath the thin fabric's shelter and pressed their ear up against their girlfriend's chest.

There it was.

That lubdub, coming down from a meaty high, yet steady, strong. November curled around her, all limbs and listening. Heather sighed and combed November's short sidecut with her long acrylics, pearlescent and studded with tiny crystals.

"Hey, so what was with that 'heartbeat' thing you were saying?" Heather asked.

November grew hot with shame. "I'm sorry. I should have discussed it with you first."

"Yeah. I mean, I get that it's your thing, and I don't mind, but just let me know if you're going to say something like that first, okay? It throws me off."

"Okay," they kept listening to her rhythm, so much steadier than their own. Her long nails combed through November's crown and they sighed.

"You should guest star on my channel." November said. "Even if just your fingernails showed up, they'd be popular."

"No, thanks! I don't want any more weirdos from your channel harassing me. I already had to set everything to private."

"Most of them are the kind of weirdos you'd like, I promise. But that's more than fair. I'm sorry that one guy harassed you like that. I still feel guilty about it."

Heather shook her head. "It's not your fault. But consider me and your audience estranged, babe."

"Mmhmm," November agreed. Their eyes were almost closed, their breathing gone deep as they stared at the slopes of their girlfriend's breasts and listened to her heartbeat.

"You're so simple. I wish I could be as simple as you are sometimes," Heather said.

"What the hell does that mean?"

"You're just satisfied with this. Listening to my heartbeat. I don't have to do anything special for you. It doesn't feel fair."

November sat up and looked at her. "You have to stay alive. That's special enough."

She made a face, a relic from some ancient adolescent phase. "Yeah, right."

"It is. And hey, sometimes you let me eat you the way I prefer." They grinned and waggled their eyebrows at her like vaudeville.

Heather laughed and let them.

It was late. Heather was tangled up in red bedding, her mouth slightly parted with subdued snores. November sat up, staring at the thin lines of Los Angeles the vertical blinds let in. The train had just gone by. But November's heart hammered in their chest with the raw, wet certainty of fear: they'd heard something. Not the train. Something bad.

They closed their eyes and tried to focus on their memory of the sound. It had a depth to it, a resonance beyond bass-heavy stereo. A sudden thought crossed their mind and they grabbed their phone to check if any earthquakes had been reported. It was after three in the morning. November glanced back at Heather, worried about waking her, but her soft snores continued on. The phone didn't offer any reassuring Richter scale anomalies.

Shaking with cold and instinct, November pulled on a *Fight! Iczer One* t-shirt and searched the apartment. It was not a long search: the bathroom and combination kitchen/office/living room space were examined in seconds. November's skin crawled but there were no prowlers hiding in the shower or behind the kitchen island. No intruders beyond the spider haunting the ZZ plant and a pair of fruit flies menacing the bananas they'd bought for breakfast.

They sat on the couch, shut their eyes, and listened.

They heard the creaks and grunts of the settling wood in the apartment building. Heather's snores interrupted as she shifted on the bed, hunting November's warmth. The muffled movement of bodies in other rooms. A distant television set playing porn at a low volume. A computer down the hall repeating sound effects of digital victory and slaughter. Water rushing through the pipes. Electricity buzzing in the power lines. Rats and opossums and squirrels and cats rustling in the bushes outside. The regular irregularity of freeway traffic.

November was ready to head back to bed when they heard it again:

A heartbeat. And then a sharp odor like hot tar.

November apologized. For the fifth time. Heather leaned over the kitchen island, her elbows carefully planted between precariously crammed kitschy ceramics and off-brand macaroni boxes, rictus-gripping her coffee cup.

"It's okay. I believe you. You heard something. And smelled something. I just can't hear it or smell it and I have to go to work in an hour and I am definitely not going back to sleep now," she said.

"I am so, so sorry," they said again.

Heather frowned. "Are you sure that you're not just chickening out? You've only been moved in for like a week now."

"Three weeks. Almost a month."

"Has it been that long?"

"Yeah."

"So is that it? Is this some cold feet sabotage?" she asked. "Be real with me for a minute."

They took a deep breath, exhaled, tried not to look at her while the words still stung. "No, this isn't about me wanting to move out."

"Or move on," she said.

"Or move on," they echoed. "I know what I heard."

"It's just all of this heartbeat shit and now I have to go to work in forty-five minutes with ninety-five percent of my stomach acid in my throat," she said, her voice croaking with leftover sleep.

"I know. I feel really bad about that."

"Good."

"Fuck you!"

"Love you, too."

She kissed November's reflexive grin.

They managed to drop Heather off at City Hall in time for work, then got caught in traffic on the way back to the apartment. They looked at the wide streets and remembered hearing that this had all been forest once, even though the only tree that they could currently see was a skinny palm a couple blocks over. It was hard to imagine. The heat pressed down like summer even though it was still early spring and not even six in the morning yet. They thought about the ozone thinning like an artery, leaking oxygen into weightless space. Oxygenated blood.

It was out of the way, but they wanted to drive by the tar pits. They hadn't been in a couple years. They turned down La Brea and then onto Wilshire, but the fence that used to give a direct view into the bubbling tar and mammoth maquettes was boarded up with either permanent or temporary construction, they couldn't tell which. They rolled down the windows and inhaled the earthy, sour tang of the tar pits beyond the plywood walls and thought about all the bones kept inside of the nearby museum over the years that had been excavated: saber-tooth and mammoth and dire wolf and even human. Remains that were usually left to decompose in peace had been pulled out of the dark and measured. Assessed. November was pretty sure the human they'd found was a murder victim; they'd gone on a field trip as a kid and that fact stuck in their mind. What had the museum called her? *L.A.'s first homicide victim*; a Tongva woman under glass for the kids to see, her bones the color of tar.

Oil and tar—the stuff their father used to call dinosaur blood. It was everywhere underneath Los Angeles. Pumpjacks still dipped and bobbed around the city like drinking bird toys, and talk of fracking could make a local either giddy or livid, depending on the local. They frowned, realizing they were near Rodeo for no good reason, and turned on the radio as they flipped back around towards their apartment. The public station had a critic on talking about a movie they didn't care much about; something with superheroes in it. They tried to follow the critique, but the lore was too complicated to unravel while driving. There was time travel in the popular franchise now, and the newest film offered dinosaurs. Dinosaur blood. November groaned.

They had to shoot a video soon and none of this was helping.

Heather used her long acrylics to tuck in the already meticulous edges of her bun. Sighed at herself. Put her hand down and resisted the urge to rub her eyes with the heel of her hand. A stack of beige folders hugged tight to her chest helped prop her torso upright. She took one of the nondescript elevators on the street down below the sidewalk, got out at a nondescript concrete and linoleum corridor, waved at the security guard she knew.

"Hey, Morales," she said.

"Hey, McRae," he said.

Down another corridor, up a level, down again, and then Heather was at work, in one of the city archive offices, the rows of files around her already reassuring with their predictability and presence. The office was a bubble of data and décor that hadn't been updated since the early 1980s. It smelled a little funky, but something Heather had learned over the years was that there was always a weird smell lurking in an office, and odors didn't dissipate easily underground.

Ellen and Witlowe were already in the back. Witlowe looked up and waved, almost knocking his thick glasses off the bridge of his nose. Heather waved back and smiled. The fluorescents hummed overhead, a kind of white noise to muffle the various sounds from the tunnels all around her.

November couldn't do fingernails the way their girlfriend could; it keyed into their gender dysphoria. But they still managed to do pretty well as a non-binary ASMR artist, even without one of the classic tools of the trade. That was because they specialized in the historical ASMR of lost experiences. Having a birdcage installed in a Victorian wig, for example, or experiencing a medieval trepanation (one of their most controversial and also most-viewed videos, despite being behind a paywall). All of their content was meticulously researched and recorded on prosumer equipment. Even though most of their videos were for paid subscribers, and a lot of their critics argued that November's harder videos could be considered pornography, the milder ones they posted on the public channels still did well and weren't usually demonetized.

They could make the rent handily if they made all of their scheduled recording and posting dates in time. But they hadn't recorded or posted in a while. Since well before the move. The dreaded ten-day gap kept on gappening, their last video scrapped when they realized their microphone had turned off halfway through recording. The video before that was ruined with intermittent leaf blowers.

November sat in their stage space, a dedicated corner of the kitchen/office/living room, fiddling with the colors of their LED fairy lights and staring at the styrofoam head they'd trepanned, when they got the text from their ex, Caroll.

R u still alive?

Probably! Why?

It's been over 20 days since ur last post. I got worried. Post something sometimes u jerk

Working on it rn. Ty for caring <3

UGH u r the worst!!!! Still hot tho

Ty!

Ur still polyam right? We should go out again. We were cute together

Polyamorous…not desperate

OUCH so mean good thing ur hot

November put their phone aside, deliberately ignoring the next cluster of incoming text message alerts that rattled against their desktop. Caroll's preoccupation with physical appearances was a big part of why they weren't dating anymore. The subject exhausted November, who thought that any adult could be considered attractive if you saw them at their most passionate or most vulnerable stages; it was the personality that coalesced around somebody's passion and vulnerability that them alluring. The cruelty or the kindness that collected there, and how it moved the flesh, that was the stuff that made November yearn to learn the secret soundtrack of someone's heart. Everything else was meat and makeup. Something to digest or wear. Temporary. And November wasn't doing hookups right now.

Not that temporary wasn't tempting sometimes.

The last three weeks hadn't gone as well as November had hoped. Most of the time lately, the easiest thing to do was let Heather decide how their evenings went. It was easier to make her happy than to try something new. Easier for them to become a tongue and follow a script than to speak up and say what they wanted. They wondered if they'd moved in with her too soon, if they should have waited longer. November felt out of practice with expressing their desires, with knowing themself, and if they were honest that was the thing killing their production schedule more than any microphone failure or leaf blower.

They wondered if Heather was right; if hearing that weird heartbeat and smelling tar in the middle of the night was some kind of subconscious sabotage. Whatever it was, they needed to talk to her. Clear the air.

They stuck their index finger through the center of the styrofoam head's hole and wiggled vigorously. Sighed.

"You and me both," they said.

The first half of Heather's day blurred by in its usual muddle of busywork and caffeine. She was reorganizing a section of city planning paperwork that hadn't been touched in decades, and it wreaked havoc on her sinuses. Dust particles floated in and out of the fluorescents. She sneezed.

A rhythm pulsed, bass-heavy and remote. The corners of old papers quivered. Heather assumed someone's over-powered stereo system was hovering over the exact wrong pipe somewhere, channeling a beat underground. She sneezed again. Heather pushed a box of files aside and searched for the packet of tissues in her purse.

A sharp odor pierced the dank archival musk. Heather's eyes watered. Her sinuses thickened with mucus. A dark glop splattered the city planning file in front of her. She blinked. It hadn't come from her nose. The strange substance appeared ink black one moment, putrescent green the next, while a slick rainbow sheen that reminded Heather of oily rain puddles constantly rippled across its surface.

"What the hell?" she said.

Heather looked around, but Witlowe and Ellen weren't nearby. She stared at the splotch on the paper in front of her, mesmerized by the peculiar quiver the bass-heavy rhythm gave it. Then a second glob fell next to the first. Heather looked up.

And darkness wetly fell.

Two large vegan leather speaker cushions cupped November's ears completely. When they turned on the noise cancellation function of their headset, the subtle background bumps and mutters in the apartment building vanished. Almost. If they focused, they could still make out bits of local noise, but the distracting stuff was gone. They closed their eyes. Listened.

November's phone buzzed with another text message notification, rattling the desk.

They sighed and turned their phone off, then put it in the bottom shelf of the desk with a definitive shove.

Inside the pulsing lubdub, not tar but tar-like goop, thick and burning, engulfed Heather's vision. She could feel its heat against the surfaces of her eyes, an inquisitive pressure, oozing around the orbs of her eyeballs, wedging between them and the sockets, sliding delicately along her optic nerves until the stuff pierced and webbed through her brain with the precision of thread-thin roots in rich soil. It was in her nose, in her throat, warmly pouring down upon her from the dusty ceiling tiles above in a baptism of unending filth.

Heather's body spasmed, her neck rocking back and forth, her grin coated in green-black rainbows. Her airways were packed full of the gunk but she was laughing. It was so warm! This wasn't a real swallowing, not a true devouring, but it felt so warm in the goop's embrace!

Lumps breached the filth's surface. A sludge-veneered dire wolf skull emerged from the pulsing muck, balancing atop the ooze as if it was regarding her. Studying the most recent acquisition in the uncertain boundary of their being.

Then its long teeth descended in a quick jawless bite.

November decided to record an episode about riding an alligator at the long-defunct California Alligator Farm. They'd researched it for months and had a lot of good notes for their efforts, even scrounged around and found a pair of real alligator skin shoes at a thrift store. Now they neatly arranged them next to a shallow dish of water. A sound board with authentic alligator sound effects cued up was at their elbow. They adjusted their camera. Checked their microphone for the fifth or sixth time. Turned on the LED ring light that gave them headaches, and put on a huge grin.

Showtime.

The first half of the recording went well. They liked being in front of the camera talking about peculiar liminal things. Having notes but going unscripted. Odd desires leaked out of the edges of different eras for different groups of people; these fads and lost convictions fascinated November. What persisted in the collective popular imagination and what became lost were frequently not different in quality, as fans often wanted to believe, but in what the present wanted to remember.

November wanted to remember everything possible. Impossible things to remember, things that had happened before November's birth, experiences lost to archives and circumstance; they wanted to know them all and understand as much as possible. To pull on the cords of desire and draw closer to the heartbeat of another human being lost in time. So they played a symphony of prerecorded hisses and live water splashes, crowd tones a chorus now supporting the solo of flesh living and dead, palm to shoe, pressed while a gator growled low.

It was good stuff. They were doing well. Then they heard it again, beneath the hiss of another alligator recording. That sound, deep and rhythmic. Pulsing. Tell-tale.

November tried to keep going. To ignore the sound. But then they stopped. Sat back and turned the microphone gain all the way up. Told themself they could edit this out of the alligator video later if they had to.

It was impossible to start a real conversation in the car ride home. Heather wouldn't look at them. Wouldn't say anything. So they waited until they got back to the apartment.

"Hey, we need to talk," November said. Then regretted it.

Heather looked like hell. Like the sleep deprivation had really done a number on her. She was usually tired after a day at work, but today she looked like she was ready to fall asleep on her feet. She stared back at November.

"About what? I don't feel like talking," she said.

"About us. It's important."

An expression rippled across Heather's face that November couldn't quite read. For a fraction of a second her eyes glittered greenly, reflected a dazzle of colors before settling into their normal brown. They frowned.

"Are you okay?"

"I'm fine. What's so important?"

She didn't sound fine.

"Well I would hope that our relationship would be important to you, in general, but in the specific I think that we rushed into things a little with me moving in, and—"

"Wow, so are you calling it quits already? What a fucking champ. Do you have somebody else lined up yet?" she said.

"Holy shit, Heather. Could you please give me a chance here?"

"Give you a chance to dump me in my own apartment? I knew I shouldn't have put you on the lease."

November's face was hot. They ran their forearm along the edges of their eyes, knocking their glasses askew as they smeared tears away.

"I wasn't—I'm not dumping you? At least I thought I wasn't? But holy crap am I starting to think that I should."

Heather opened her mouth to talk but retched up a font of green-black iridescence instead. November stared at her blankly. A piercing, oily odor stung the air. Their girlfriend sagged to her knees.

"Oh my god, Heather!" November caught her before the back of her head could hit the kitchen island. "You're sick—no wonder you're feeling like shit. Don't worry. It's going to be okay, it's going to be okay," they repeated to her, their soft arms trembling with Heather's weight, adrenaline pressing their heartrate like a button.

Ellen turned off the last row of fluorescent lights in the archive office, selected the correct key from her keyring and locked up, then waved good night to the security guard down the hall as he turned the corner. A subtle pulse, rhythmic and steady, vibrated the walls. The old white woman hardly noticed. Ellen headed down the linoleum hall in the direction of the elevator bank but paused when she heard something behind her. A heavy, wet clatter she didn't understand. Ellen looked back. The linoleum ended in a set of double doors that were propped open and locked into the floor. Beyond that were the long, square service tunnels meandering underneath the street. Periodic fluorescent strip lights buzzed down the pipe-lined tunnels. Nothing out of the ordinary was there.

The sixty-two-year-old woman released the breath that fear had caught for her and turned back to the elevators.

Iridescent darkness engulfed her from above.

"We need to go to the emergency room," November said.

"We can't afford the emergency room," Heather said.

Heather was in bed early. November sat on the bed next to her. A fresh glass of cold water beaded with condensation on the cluttered red nightstand nearby.

"That doesn't matter. You have insurance," they said.

"My insurance is crap and barely covers anything and you know it."

"We can try to make it work."

Heather shook her head. "That's a fantasy. You're almost out of money right now, and I'm not much better."

"Okay but just…will you do me the favor and call, at least? Just call the doctor and see what the copay is. I'll cover it. Don't worry about how."

Heather stared at them. Her eyes watered. She swallowed thickly.

"Okay, I'll call the doctor. Hey, No? I'm sorry. Really, really sorry. I don't know what's wrong with me. I just…it's like everything that's been building up over the past month fell out of me all at once."

"Yeah, and it's on our carpet," they said.

"Ha. You know what I mean. Angry shit. I'm sorry for dumping it all on you," she said.

"Thanks for the apology."

"What were you trying to tell me?"

"It's not that important right now," they said.

"It is," she said.

November folded their arms across their chest. "Okay. Well. I haven't been feeling like I can tell you what I want lately. Ever since I moved in."

"Like about sex?"

"Like about everything. Like about what we're going to have for dinner or watch on television or do on the weekends," they said.

"I thought that you liked it when I make decisions for you. You knew how I felt about being in control when you moved in," she said.

"Sometimes I do like it. Sometimes it's hot and it makes me feel like you care. But knowing that you're listening to me is the care I really need from a partner, Heather."

A flicker passed over Heather's face. Her eyes sparkled with shadows. "I know what you really need you fucking—"

November nearly missed passing the plastic paint bucket over in time to catch the hot plumes of green-black sludge spewing from Heather's mouth. An inexplicable reek that November could only mentally label as "rotten motor oil" filled the bedroom. Gently they held Heather's hair away from her face as a fresh gout of goop jerked up her throat.

Heather kept saying she was fine, but November insisted she take a sick day. She tried to debate them about it but her debate was cut short by another episode of vomiting. She took the sick day.

November made Heather oatmeal and tea for breakfast and watched her make an appointment with her doctor over the phone. The copay was pricey, but they could manage it. Barely. Once they saw her eating a couple spoonfuls of oatmeal, November left her alone to edit the alligator video in the kitchen/office/living room.

It was difficult to focus on editing. Their mind kept wandering. One video wasn't going to be enough to solve all of their problems, and it felt inexplicably irresponsible to be working instead of taking care of their girlfriend. The hours crawled by, and every sound that came from the bedroom made them want to check on her. But Heather wasn't calling for help. When the final set of edits finished rendering, and the export seemed to be clean, November felt as physically exhausted as the time they'd run a marathon in high school without eating breakfast. Like an empty sack on legs, even though they'd eaten a banana and half a cheese sandwich after getting Heather oatmeal that morning.

November opened up a new file. Stared at the screen. Thought about the heartbeat again. They selected the raw video clip of the alligator footage, then scrubbed over to the point where the weird sound began. Listened.

It was a heartbeat. Distinctly organic. Steady. Rhythmic. Subtle but impossibly vast. The kind of sound that should not be coming from the ground.

The clip ended abruptly with the microphone cutting out. They played it again. Closed their eyes. They wanted to be afraid of the sound, but they weren't. They licked their dry bottom lip.

The retching sounds from the bedroom were suddenly so intense that November pulled their left headset speaker cushion askew and stood up. As they turned to look the bedroom door flew open, Heather a blur, vomiting into the paint bucket she death-gripped while dashing into the bathroom. They pulled the headset off, ran over and banged on the locked door.

"Heather? Are you okay? Heather?"

Heather didn't turn on the bathroom light. She didn't want to look. She knelt over the bathtub in the dark, unbelievable amounts of goo wetly pouring out of her to join the slowly-draining muck she'd dumped out from the bucket. A nightmare, perpetually bending her body against her will. She just wanted it to end.

But not when she closed her eyes.

Now her eyes slammed shut and the feeling rippled over her body again; inch by square inch the stuff oozed out of her pores, warmly reclaiming her skin for its own. Glittering and green. She moaned with pleasure.

The impossible thing knew what she liked. They had promised to give her what she wanted. A real swallowing. She trembled with the promise of it.

She heard November's voice muffled through the bathroom door, asking Heather if she was okay. She wished she knew.

The doctor's office that took Heather's insurance was in a building with noticeable structural damage. Pieces of the building were missing or stained, the first two address numbers in the sign facing the street the most obvious victims of neglect. November drove, parking in a narrow lot behind the building that hadn't had its parking stripes repainted in at least a couple decades. They took their best guess and parked in a spot far away from the other two vehicles in the lot—a shapeless sedan and a BMW from the late 1980s with a dusty car cover half pulled over it. When they got out of their compact the smell of lunch from the Korean restaurant next door hit them, and November perked up.

"Hey I might go grab something from the place next door when this is over. How does that sound?"

Heather looked at them from over the rim of the paint bucket. "You selfish—"

They sighed as Heather emptied herself into the bucket again.

The waiting room was crowded—not a single chair remained open. A couple of young black children restlessly flapped the pages of outdated magazines like wings. Everyone recoiled from Heather and her paint bucket. A few people put their hands over their noses and mouths. One

Latinx man tucked his nose underneath the collar of his t-shirt and kept it pinched in place.

"But you said over the phone that you took her insurance," November was saying to the receptionist.

"I'm sorry, but we don't accept this provider. You can call the number on the card and try to—"

Heather retched another wet stream of sludge into the bucket. A few people made noises of disgust. When she finished she turned to the receptionist, her chin like rave makeup gone rank.

"You can tell the doctor to go fuck herself. She's never done a goddamn thing except push free samples down my throat," she said.

"Heather, stop that. I know you're not feeling well but they're not the problem."

Heather turned to November. They recoiled at the oily shadows in her eyes. "Not the problem? Are you kidding me? They're all the problem."

"It's the insurance company's—"

"Shut up!"

"We're going to have to ask you to leave, ma'am," said the receptionist, a veneer of cop entering her tone.

"Please," they said, "can't you ask the doctor to just take a look? She's seen Heather before."

"No, and frankly, Heather should be in the emergency room."

"We can't afford the emergency room," November said.

A white security guard entered the waiting room, holding his belt importantly as he stood by the door. He had pepper spray secured in a holster at his hip. He unbuttoned the little leather restraining strap that kept the cannister secured.

"Look at this big brave asshole. What are you going to do, pepper spray a sick person?" Heather sneered.

"Only if you don't leave, ma'am," he said.

"Come on, Heather, let's go," November said.

"Fine," Heather said. She started walking towards the door. Relieved, November followed. As Heather approached the security guard she smiled at him. His features crumpled in disgust and he reached for his pepper spray.

"Oh, don't act like this isn't already inside of you," she said to him, and tossed the contents of the paint bucket at him.

Everyone screamed. The horrible, oily stink filled the tiny room. Iridescent sludge slithered down him, from his scalp to his stomach. The security guard, flailing and unable to see, tried to shoot his pepper spray but couldn't get a proper grip on the cannister and it fell to the floor in a sticky splotch.

November frowned; they saw something that didn't make sense. Something beyond the weird comic violence of what was unfolding in front of them. Something small, but irresolvable.

"Come on, let's go," Heather said to them.

They followed her, trying to understand why the green-black goop had wriggled up into the security guard's ear canals like earthworms seeking the soil of his flesh, hardly hearing the screams behind them as they took the elevator down to the car.

They drove home still puzzling over this mystery. Heather seemed better than she'd been all morning; she sat up and fiddled with the car radio buttons, making faces at the pop songs she didn't like. It was only when they got home that November remembered about lunch and the Korean restaurant and they sighed aloud at the thought of the tteokbokki they'd missed out on.

"What's wrong?" Heather asked.

They blinked. "Everything, I guess."

She shrugged. "That's good, right? It means that nothing can get any worse."

"I guess."

But things got worse.

"I want to play with you tonight," Heather said.

"Are you sure you're feeling well enough?" November asked. "You were really sick this morning—"

"I haven't thrown up since we got home. Come on, I want to play."

"Okay. But we stop if you feel sick at all. Like, *at all*. Little Red Riding Hood again?"

"Not this time. I wrote a new script," she said.

"Really? When did you have time to write a new script?"

"I wrote it while you were editing this morning. Come on. Just read it."

November glanced at the script that their girlfriend handed them. Their printer was out of black ink so the script's type had taken on an indigo hue. They briefly scanned the text, then looked up from it.

"I don't want to do this," November said.

"Come on, at least read it first. You didn't give yourself enough time to read it."

"I *am* reading it," they said.

It was written in a kind of simplified playwriting format that Heather always used when she wrote the scripts that they performed together.

WHAT ATE THE ANGELS

BEDROOM—all candles lit. N completely clothed, wearing dark clothing (style up to N but more formal/dressy preferred). H completely unclothed. Bucket and plastic syringe (no needle) are nearby.

N: I'm so hungry. I have consumed cities, planets, gods and universes, but still I hunger. I want you. I crave you.

H: Who are you? Why do you want me?

N: No one has ever named me. My blood is the blood of legion. My voice is the voice of the dead. I am the devourer of mortals. Eater of stones. I am the one that ate this city's angels. I am the one who will watch this world's sun die and eat its cold corpse.

H: Unnamed thing, why do you want me?

N: I crave your sweetness. It calls to me. The promise of your flavor. I want to eat your joy. Your sorrow. I want to empty your husk of its meat and replace it with my divine liquidity.

H spreads legs wide on bed.

H: Then fill me with your divinity.

N takes the plastic syringe to the bucket, sucks up holy fluid into the syringe's barrel, slowly injects contents of the syringe into H vaginally.

November put down the script. "Okay, I read it. I'm still not doing it."

Heather's eyes gave a green-black glint. "Are you fucking Caroll again?"

November covered their mouth. "What?"

"You heard me."

"I don't even understand why you would say that."

"Quit avoiding the question. Is that why you won't play with me? Because you're getting it from your ex? Don't lie to me."

Shocked tears streaked down November's face. "I wouldn't cheat on you. I've always been honest with you."

"So why can't you tell me that you're not fucking Caroll?"

They stared at Heather, whose eyes glittered in the dark of the apartment.

"I'm not fucking Caroll," they said.

"Are you sure?"

"Jesus, Heather. I know you're sick, but I don't know if I can take this."

"Take what?"

"Are you kidding? You've been acting weird ever since you came home from work."

"You're the one that's been acting weird, November. Ever since you moved in."

"For fuck's sake, Heather, that's not the same! I want to be able to express myself, you want me to shoot mystery vomit up your cunt!"

"You know I hate that word!"

"I give up," they said.

"What do you mean?"

"This argument. I surrender. I apologize. I didn't want to insult you or fight you or anything."

"Good. I accept your apology. I'll give you half an hour to memorize your lines."

"No," November said, "you don't get it. I'm not doing this with you."

"What are you talking about?"

"I'm not participating in this—whatever the hell you're doing. I'm going out."

"What do you mean by 'out'? Where the fuck are you going?"

"Out is what I mean by 'out'. I'm taking my car."

Heather started to insult them but a fresh swell of liquid swam up her throat. She ran to the bathroom. November listened to her throw up for a while, then realized they couldn't keep listening to her anymore. They grabbed their keys, shoving the guilt they felt about leaving Heather alone while she was sick roughly aside as they headed out the door.

96

November cried over their steering wheel for a while, not driving, just slumped over sobbing in their seat. They let everything fall out of them, until their sinuses ached and their eyes felt bruised. They didn't know what to do, but they knew they needed help.

November cleaned the lenses of their tear-spotted glasses on the corner of their Orville Peck t-shirt. They decided in that moment to go see Caroll. Horny, dependable Caroll. November searched their pockets for their phone, intending to text ahead, until they remembered that they'd left it inside the desk upstairs. Upstairs, where they didn't want to be right now.

They turned on the ignition and headed out.

The sunset was giving an encore before it went offstage for the night; streaks of magenta and gold came from the coast. The rest was dark desert blue. They drove to Culver City. Stopped on the way at a weed dispensary to purchase a half gram vape pen. Navigated to their apartment and found parking on the street about a block away—not bad for the city at this hour.

The buzzer to Caroll's apartment wasn't working, so they had to wait until another tenant let them into the building. It was a busy night. They didn't have to wait long.

"Wow, hey, what's going on November?"

Caroll stood in the open doorway of their apartment. They looked so concerned that November almost started crying again, but didn't. November held up the vape pen. "I need to smoke this while you listen to me lose my mind for about twenty minutes. Sound good?"

Caroll held their front door open a little wider, revealing precisely how unironed their button up and cargo pants were. "I always have time for the problems of gorgeous people."

November rolled their eyes and went inside.

Caroll listened attentively to the whole story without interrupting. Even the part with the sludge worming its way into the security guard's ears. The only part that November omitted was the specific contents of Heather's play.

"What did she want you to do?"

"It's just…it was not in my comfort zone. Let's just say that."

"Okay. Interesting," Caroll said.

"Why is that interesting?"

"Because you're comfortable with a lot of freaky shit."

"Right. Any other insights?" November asked them.

"I mean this sounds like classic movie monster crap, right? Sludge worms in somebody's brain? Are you sure you didn't watch something while on an edible?"

"This vape is the only weed I've had in over a month," November said.

"Well, option two is, and I hate to say it because you're not going to like hearing this, but this sounds just like a lot of toxic behavior coming from her. Insulting you, trying to control you. Maybe this was waiting to come out once she got comfortable."

"Maybe. But she used to be better at communicating with me. Something's in the way. It's like she doesn't care about what I have to say at all anymore," November said.

"Yeah. The thing in the way is her own bullshit, and it's not up to you to fix her."

"I don't know, Caroll, maybe you're right."

"About Heather being toxic? I know I'm right," Caroll said.

"Maybe it's it *is* classic movie monster crap," November said.

"What?"

"You said it yourself—sludge worms going into people's ears aren't normal, right? And Heather started acting weird after going to work. Well, she works in a bunch of tunnels underneath City Hall. Who knows what kind of weird shit that's connected to? The heartbeat sound is real, too. I have it on a flash drive. And the gross stuff that's coming out of Heather is real."

"Give me the vape," Caroll said.

"Why?"

"Because you have me half convinced and I refuse to be sober and believe in this shit."

November passed them the vape pen. "I think she's really sick. Infected with something. I don't know what it is, but I want to help her."

Caroll exhaled a deep toke. "It's not your job to save her, November."

"Then who's going to do it? Her family cut her out years ago, and her two closest friends stopped talking to her ever since she started dating me because I'm going to somehow ruin her by getting too much poly or bi or non-binary on her—I don't know which anymore."

"Sounds like they were shit friends."

"I'll be the first to say it—they *are* shit friends. They know that she isn't on social media, and they haven't texted her in weeks now. So who else has she got?"

"All right, November, jeez. You can play the hero if you want to."

"I don't want to be a hero. I just want to have a girl-friend I can cuddle up to at night, or if I can't have that, at least another ex that I know is going to survive after I move out at the end of next month."

"Ugh," Caroll said, "you're disgustingly hot when you're trying to not be the hero."

November flipped them off, but smiled a little.

November needed time to sober up before they could drive, so they asked to borrow Caroll's computer. They sat in front of the stickerbombed laptop. Wacky horror movie logic. Fine. It made no sense to go along with it, but the heartbeat made no sense. The oil made no sense. The script that Heather had written made no sense.

So they searched online like a *Scooby Doo* hero: for information about the tar pits, the tunnels, everything and anything they could think of related to the weirdness that had been going on recently. They discovered the tunnels had been dug during the Prohibition era, physically connecting illegal speakeasies directly with the corrupt politicians that publicly rallied against them. The political corruption was interesting, a fascinating part of Los Angeles history, but they couldn't see how it connected to Heather's sickness.

November put aside the tunnel research and focused on the tar pits. They learned oil was made out of pressurized rotting organic material. Dying things or the dead. The only living entities that were currently known to be capable of surviving in a tar pit were bacteria. November remembered the green patina to the oily muck that Heather had been vomiting. A cartoonish clue: *that felt right*. They kept reading.

Bacteria. The stuff that vastly outnumbered human cells inside every human body. Most bacteria was useful, or at the very least harmless, but a few varieties were known to cause disease. November became absorbed. Emailed themselves a few links. When they finally checked the time they cursed aloud—three in the morning—a lot later than they'd planned on being out. They went to go thank Caroll but found them asleep on the couch, snoring through their open mouth. They left without waking them.

November tried to enter the apartment as quietly as possible. The rotten tar smell had intensified; it was so strong their eyes stung and began to water as soon as they opened the door. The light connected to the switch by the front door wouldn't turn on. They flipped it up and down a few times, but the filament in the overhead bulb of the kitchen/office/living room remained dark.

"Heather? Are you home?"

Nobody answered. November figured she was asleep, like most reasonable people in Los Angeles at that hour. They stood in the dark, waiting to move until their eyes adjusted to the faint amount of light that filtered into the room through the vertical blinds at night.

That was when they realized Heather was only a few feet away, sitting at their desk.

They screamed—a quick, vestigial gut-shriek of confronting eyes in the dark—but Heather didn't react. She just sat there, staring at them. November pressed the knuckles of their fist against their own racing heartrate.

"Wow! I guess you waited up for me. I'm sorry. You shouldn't have," they said.

"Where were you?"

They hesitated before they spoke. "I went to go talk to Caroll."

"Interesting. They just keep coming up, don't they?"

"You knew that they would. They're not just an ex, they're a good friend of mine."

"A 'good friend', huh? Okay, No, I'm going to ask you one last time: Are you cheating on me?"

With that emotional blow, all of November's deferred fatigue came for them at once. They sagged on their feet, staring sadly at their girlfriend.

"Heather, for the last time, please, I'm not cheating on you. You're afraid right now, all of this is fear, but that's okay, it's going to pass. We can get you help."

Heather held November's phone up. "So you're saying that you're not fucking Caroll? Tell me something believable."

November squinted at the screen, a rectangle lit up to reveal the scroll of flirty text messages Caroll had sent them earlier.

"Do you honestly think I'm back together with them just because they sent me a bunch of horny crap? Come on, Heather, I know you know me better than that."

Heather groaned, the sound terminating somewhere deep in her throat into plosives like bubbles popping. "I don't know," she said. "I don't know that."

"Yes, you do."

"Play with me, November. Just shut up and play with me."

"Heather, listen to me, please. This isn't you. This is the infection talking."

"An infection can't talk."

They stepped towards her. A trilling purr bubbled mucous-thick in the back of Heather's throat.

"I think you're experiencing a side effect, Heather. A very sophisticated side effect of a bacteria that usually lives inside of oil veins and tar pits," they said.

"A side effect? What do they mean by 'a side effect'?" she repeated to herself. "Is a soul a side effect? Maybe it is."

They took another step forward. Now she retreated a step.

"I think that the bacteria is stimulating a bunch of toxic stuff inside of your brain, maybe trying to change you, the chemicals of you, so that it can continue to live inside of you. But you don't have to become what it wants you to be."

Heather shook her head. "Too late."

They stepped forward again. She retreated.

"No, Heather, it's just bacteria. We can get you an antibiotic."

Heather screamed, an unexpected stream of oily vomit accompanied the sound—November barely avoided it in time.

But November reached their desk. And more importantly, to their laptop, asleep but soon awake with a flutter of fingertips across the keyboard. They yanked out their headset cord and hit play on the heartbeat clip.

The rhythmic throb utilized all the bass in the laptop's readymade speakers. Heather froze, staring at the computer. In the light of its screen November saw glittering darkness bloom in patches across their girlfriend's skin, oozing pinprick-small from her pores until every exposed cell was covered with the rancid stuff.

"No, no," Heather said, dripping onto the carpet. "not yet! You promised!"

Heather tried to scrape the stuff off of her arms, splattering it everywhere.

"Not yet!" she screamed. "Not yet!"

November turned off the playback. The heartbeat sound cut out immediately. Heather was sobbing, still struggling to clean the oily sludge off of herself. November frowned, not sure if they'd done the right thing. Heather's sobs were deep, mournful. At least the stuff didn't seem to be leaking out of her anymore.

November helped their girlfriend get into the shower, then into bed. Sleep was a blackout that November spent on the couch. When they woke up the next morning and checked in on Heather she was asleep, tangled up in her red sheets with strands of green-black goop drooling from the corners of her mouth. November frowned.

Heather looked worse, her pale skin blotched with purple bruises beneath the surface. And there were teeth in the bucket by the bed.

The teeth looked human as far as November could tell, but they weren't about to go fishing around in the goop to find out. November crouched by Heather, peering into her parted mouth. The teeth that they could see all looked like they were still in place. Nothing obvious missing from Heather's set. They were about to get up but hesitated. It had been a while since they'd been this close to Heather. And they could hear it—the heartbeat.

Not her heartbeat, not Heather's heartbeat—the other one. Only instead of coming from deep below the ground, it was coming from Heather's chest.

November leaned in; close, closer. They craned their ear forward to her breastbone, pressed it to the flesh there. Closed their eyes in ecstasy.

The sound was like music, so deep, so compelling and resonant that they wanted to listen to it play on forever. An arcane melody, primal and comforting. A cellular song, hungry for decay. If November stayed like that, listening, they were certain they would begin to understand so much.

"Did they make you a promise, too?" Heather asked them.

November woke up on the couch. Stripes of sunlight cooked the rotten oil stains on the carpet of the kitchen/office/living room. Their skull throbbed with a fresh headache.

"Heather?"

They got up and searched the apartment, but she was gone.

Morales was the only security guard on the floor. The fluorescents buzzed their endless drone above him. The Latinx man scrolled through a social media app on his phone, chuckling low to himself when he saw a funny video of a cat that had a face exactly like his brother-in-law's. He was in the middle of sending the video to his sister when he heard a loud, oddly wet sound. He froze and looked down the brightly-lit hall.

"Who's there?" he asked.

It was Heather McRae—one of the government archivists. Morales relaxed, but only a little. Heather's stance was off, her legs uncomfortably angled so that she looked like she might topple over any minute. He wondered if she was drunk.

"Hey, maybe it's time to head home tonight, McRae," he said.

"I am heading home," she said. And ropes of oily jade darkness rushed at him from the center of her being.

Heather walked down the fluorescent hallway, past the gagging, dying man, into the labyrinthine poured concrete tunnels beyond. The iridescent filth followed close at her heel with all the fawning devotion of a pet.

November rifled through their medicine cabinet. Pill bottles and antibiotic ointment and a dusty menstrual cup fell to the floor. They got on their hands and knees and checked all the labels of the prescription bottles, flinging aside the ones that didn't meet their approval.

"Damnit, damnit, damnit!" November sat up quickly and hit the back of their head against the bottom of the bathroom sink. "DAMNIT!"

From the living room, the buzz of November's phone announced an incoming text message. Probably another one from Carroll. November sighed and rubbed the back of their head. Not a single antibiotic in the apartment.

Another buzz. November scrambled to their feet and ran to get their phone.

The tunnels underneath the streets echoed with the racket from above. Heather had long left the well-lit corridors of fluorescents and poured concrete behind, her filth a constant companion. Now she was in rougher passages, the walls and ceilings often no more than raw stone and dirt.

The tunnel ahead branched. Heather followed the feeling in her gut that tugged her forward, towards her promised ending. Her swallowing. She went down the right fork. Her feet moved confidently in the darkness.

Suddenly she stopped and ran her hands along the rough rock until she found it—a door in the middle of the stone wall. An old-fashioned door, the kind you might find on a building from the 1920s or '30s. Splinters from the old wood bit her palm, her fingertips. Still she groped the door in the dark, searching for the handle.

Heather's hand finally found the knob and turned. The space inside was dim, but still brighter than the tunnels. A subaural pulse buzzed the floor, the walls. Confidently, she entered the room.

November stared at the pharmacist. "Can't you just give me, like, some amoxicillin? I'll pay you for it."

"Like I said, you need a prescription in order for me to give you that antibiotic," she said.

"I can't get a prescription at the moment."

"Then I'm sorry but I just can't help you. Could you please step out of the line?"

"Come on! It's not like I'm asking for vancomycin or anything."

November's phone buzzed in their pocket. They took it out and glanced at the screen. Caroll had gotten back to them.

I don't have anything like that atm but my friend Kelsey had a UTI and they said they have some extra cipro

They included a photo of Kelsey's prescription bottle. November smiled, texted them back.

Now whos the hero??? thnx Caroll! pls tell Kelsey I OWE THEM ONE

November had never taken the elevators down to the archives before. They knew that they weren't supposed to be there, and if a security guard spotted them, they had no real plan other than to run. It wasn't a good plan.

They tried to remember the directions to the archives. The elevator led them down to a level reminiscent of an empty hospital corridor. All greenish lighting and linoleum. Their adrenaline kept them grit-teethed, taut. They walked around until they found the escalator bank, started running when they realized that nobody was in sight, and went up a level. Down again.

The rotten tar smell was getting stronger. November glanced up and saw green-black iridescence clinging to the ceiling tiles like mold. They followed the trail of filth with their eyes. The goop above lead to a utility door, propped open and locked into the floor.

The concrete tunnels were there, on the other side of that door.

November took a deep breath and followed the sludge's trail.

It was so dark that November had to use their phone's flashlight to light the way. Rocks and pipes and the occasional rat popped up in their portable halo. Whenever the tunnel branched November closed their eyes and listened.

The heartbeat was there; faint but buzzing like a beacon and getting louder with every step they took towards it. Pulsing in the floor. The walls. Promising eternal comfort.

November went down the right fork. Kept walking for a while. They saw an old door in the middle of a rough rock wall, slightly ajar. They pushed it open.

It was slightly lighter in the space beyond the door. It took November a moment to recognize the room as the inside of an old speakeasy, its remaining tables and chairs stacked and shoved up against the walls.

What was inside of the speakeasy was far less easy to recognize.

The green-black goop was abundant; it filled the room in lumpy mounds that oozed skulls and tibias and fingerbones from its peaks. Ellen was there, her torso canted like a candle sagging in a heap of moldy icing. Morales was planted in the muck alongside her. The security guard from the doctor's office. Various people that November didn't know or recognize studded the filth, too. These strangers smiled at November, reached towards them, but could not leave the points where their torsos were secured.

Then November saw Heather.

She wasn't planted in the oily muck—yet. She was approaching the vast mouth of an impossible being. Eyeless, earless, the green-black filth formed a maw atop a shifting pile. Its snout was long and iridescent, slightly taller than Heather and at least twice as long, and when the orifice opened it revealed a tongue like a living mattress and teeth made of broken femurs that fit together in perfect dental occlusion.

Heather looked so happy. She was covered in filth but they'd never seen her look so happy before. And the heartbeat was there, throbbing so hard that November could feel it through the soles of their shoes, promising comfort, promising the connection that November kept hunting through their ASMR performances, but this connection was happening now, poignant and truly, uniquely unforgettable.

"Heather, I can't give you anything like that," November said loudly. They weren't sure if she heard at first, but Heather looked back at them. November walked into the room, their boots squelching in the muck, avoiding the hands of the strangers that reached for them.

"I can't fulfill that fantasy for you, and I wouldn't, because I'm not a monster. I don't believe in using you up like that. And you shouldn't, either," they said.

"Why not?" Heather was crying, sending streaks through the green-black iridescence on her face.

"Because you're not a monster, either."

Heather's sobs came harder, deeper from her chest. "What if I am?"

The heartbeat expanded its aural volume with every throb, tempting in its intensity. November could feel it quiver in the bones of their hips, in the tender inner parts of their ears. The tongue lolled out of the giant mouth, its tip wrapped around Heather's calf.

"You can stop being one," they said.

Heather's eyes sparkled darkly. "It's already inside of me. You said that I'm infected, so why not let it take the rest of me?"

November approached her, a lopsided smile on their face. "You're thinking in a binary—it eats you and you die or it doesn't eat you and I try to save you. What if you let the thing eat you and I try to save you?"

"What?" Confusion wrinkled glittery green on Heather's brow.

"Hell, I want to check out this thing's heartbeat up close, how about we go in together—would you mind that?"

"I don't know what—wait, how—"

November held up Kelsey's bottle of ciprofloxacin and popped off the cap. "I've been inhaling and touching this oily crap for days now, I'm sure that I'm already exposed to the same bacteria you are. Split this bottle of antibiotics with me. Then let's do it."

Heather stepped out of the green-black tongue's embrace and held November, squeezing them tightly.

"Really? You're willing to do this with me?" she said.

"Of course." They dry-swallowed half of the pills, then passed the rest to Heather. "You know that I'm into a lot of freaky shit."

Heather laughed, then tried to do the same dry-swallow with her mouthful of antibiotics. When she struggled to get them down November held her still and kissed her, easing their saliva into her dirty mouth tongue-first, then slowly down her bacteria-coated throat. Soon she was able to swallow, but even when the pills were gone they remained connected like that for a while.

When they finally broke apart, November's eyes were thick with green-black iridescence. Heather smiled at them and they grinned back at her. Held her hand.

On the count of three, they jumped together.

The upper set of teeth snapped down and they fell, spinning, swimming through pulsing black rainbows that pressed warm around them, and they kept her close to their heart, far from the teeth, unconcerned about anything for a few minutes except how good it felt to throb in the dark with her.

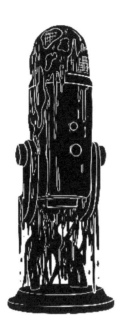

ABOUT THE AUTHORS

CYNTHIA GÓMEZ is a writer and researcher living in Oakland. She writes horror and speculative fiction and has a particular love for themes of revenge, retribution, and resistance to oppression. She has stories in *The Acentos Review*, *Strange Horizons*, and the anthology *Antifa Splatterpunk*. You can find her on Twitter at @cynthiasaysboo.

M. LOPES DA SILVA (he/they/she) is a non-binary and bisexual author from Los Angeles. They write pulp and poetry, and sometimes the two get mixed up together. Their queer California horror fiction has been published or is forthcoming from *In Somnio: A Collection of Modern Gothic Horror Fiction*, *Antifa Splatterpunk*, and *Stories of the Eye*. Unnerving Magazine previously published their debut novella *Hooker:* a pro-queer, pro-sex work, feminist retrowave pulp thriller about a bisexual sex worker hunting a serial killer in 1980s Los Angeles using hooks as her weapons of choice.

ABOUT THE ARTISTS

C. PAUL RAMEY is an illustrator based in Philadelphia, PA. They work mostly in black and white, and use traditional tools such as dip pens and inkwells to make contemporary compositions with an old-fashioned aura. They are inspired mostly from Victorian ghost stories, and artists like Edward Gorey, Stephen Gammel, and Junji Ito. You can find more of their work, and original stories on Twitter @mathraptor42.

EVANGELINE GALLAGHER is an award-winning illustrator from Baltimore, Maryland. They received their BFA in Illustration from the Maryland Institute College of Art in 2018. When they aren't drawing they're probably hanging out with their dog, Charlie, or losing at a board game. They possess the speed and enthusiasm of 10,000 illustrators.

ACKNOWLEDGMENTS

CYNTHIA GÓMEZ – A story has so many little midwives, and this story has many. LP Kindred and Eric Raglin: I run out of grateful words for the way your guidance shaped this story into what it is now. Thea Boodhoo: I remember spending an entire afternoon talking with you about this piece. If attention is one of the best gifts we can give each other, I'm so spoiled.

Thank you to the folks in the San Francisco Writers Workshop, especially to Olga Zilberbourgh and Judy Viertel, whose affection for this story was so encouraging. Thank you to my group at Tin House 2019 and to Justin Torres for your leadership, and for the praise you wrote that I open up and reread when I need to. Micah Clatterbaugh, you said, "How about you *write* the stories you keep talking about?" Pues, here it is.

And I love my family, who reads every fucking thing I write. From the time I was writing it in crayon. If it's been days or years since I've seen you, if you're close or far away. Mama, Papa, and Big Sister bear, and all the others too. Abrazos fuertes y gracias por todo todito.

M. LOPES DA SILVA – I'd like to thank all of the people who helped this little story about messy queers come to life: Samantha Mayotte and Shelley Lavigne, who read first and helped the angels sing; Mae Murray and all of the HWSG members for their support of my angels; William Bibbiani for loving and caffeinating the angels; Alex Ebenstein for taking a chance on my angels; and Lor Gislason for the goop.

CPSIA information can be obtained
at www.ICGtesting.com
Printed in the USA
BVHW031301011122
650802BV00008B/155